Emanuela La Capricciosa

THE COLORS OF

SEDUCTION

PROLOGUE

I was deep in my thought and surrounded by the smoke of my cigarette when an irresistible impulse gripped my brain and my soul. I had to see him. I carefully chose my dress; a sheath dress whose length allowed the lace of the hold-up tights to become visible; I put cigarettes and a lighter in my bag and went out into the sticky air of the midsummer night. He was sitting at his usual bar table, melancholically sipping his drink.

«Can I have a light?» I asked him, the unlit cigarette between my lips. The flame lit up my face and ignited not only the aromatic stick, but all my senses. Our respective fantasies rose, flew high, to end up on a bed, between fresh sheets and languid caresses. Then, we came back to reality.

«Thank you!» I said carelessly, moving away amidst clouds of smoke exhaled in the humidity of the night.

Leaving a man in the throes of desire makes me feel victorious, I come home with a strange taste in my mouth, I almost feel like I can sense the rancor and resentment he feels for me. And, usually, it makes me feel good.

But not that night, that night I lost. I still had his eyes printed in my mind. I retraced my steps, took him by the hand without uttering a word. The urge to possess him and let him possess me was too strong to reach a bed. We conquered a dark corner of the street and let our senses run free.

When I emerged from the dullness of my senses, which I had to thank for being due to a pleasure rarely experienced at other times, I realized that he was no longer there, he had disappeared. I was alone in the darkness of the night.

The roar of the waves could be heard distinctly in the silence. In the distance, the sound of the siren of a ship approaching the port. On my skin, sticky with moisture, I could still smell his skin. I smelled it with pleasure and found in me the present memory of the passion that had overwhelmed us. I got up, I rearranged the crumpled dress with my hands and, rocking on my stiletto heels, I reached the square illuminated by the languid light of the streetlamps. I stretched my pace; I couldn't wait to reach the bed: I was exhausted. I entered the darkness of the alley on my right and climbed the steps leading to the door. I had finally arrived. I only took off my shoes and then, without even undressing, I fell asleep on the sheets.

I was awakened by the repeated ringing of my cell phone, which rang inside my bag at the foot of the bed. The morning light had flooded the room and I had to squint to avoid being dazzled. I remained motionless in bed, heedless of the sound. I already knew who it was, and I had no intention of moving even a muscle to hear that voice. I turned on my side and smiled smugly.

CHAPTER 1

Monday, Red, Envy

August was ending, taking with it the memories of summer and vacation. The day was clear, and it would be hot, even if in Recanati, a town perched on a hill facing the Adriatic and a short distance from it, it was difficult to suffer the heat even in the middle of summer. A fresh north wind or mistral winds swept the streets and squares of the town all year round, making the atmosphere pleasant in that season, much less so on grey winter days.

The imposing statue of Leopardi cast its shadow right at the little table of the bar in the square where I, known to everyone in town as Emanuela "La capricciosa", was having my breakfast, a croissant with Chantilly cream and cappuccino with a nice sprinkling of cocoa. That shadow was reminding me and all the other inhabitants of what Recanati was known for all over Italy and perhaps all over the world. Usually a beautiful and lonely forty-year-old woman needs only a gesture to attract even the shyest of men to her, but not in that "native wild village" where everyone knows everyone's life, death, and everything in between. I would have turned forty the following November; as a child I always reproached my parents for having conceived me to be born in the month of the dead, but now I didn't care anymore. From the viewpoint of the observer, my green eyes stood out in contrast with my hair, made even darker than its natural color thanks to the work of a skilled hairdresser. I wore a little red dress, cinched at the waist by a black belt and held up at the shoulder by thin straps, which revealed my delicate skin, only slightly ambered by my summer tan. The lower end of the dress didn't reach the knee so, while sitting, my legs, veiled by light summer tights almost invisible, were fully showing. The scarlet color of the lipstick matched a red rose that the waiter had placed in a thin glass vase in the center of the table. I wouldn't have given up my breakfast at the bar for anything in the world before going to work at the travel agency in Corso Persiani, where I was returning after three wonderful weeks of vacation. Gathering the foam from the cappuccino with a spoon not to leave my favorite thing in the cup, I pulled a cigarette out of the packet and stuck it in my mouth. I spent some time looking for the lighter in my bag, pretending not to find it, even though I could feel it and was even clutching it in the palm of my hand. Usually, soon someone would approach me to offer me a light; I had gotten used to it in the tourist village in Puglia where I had stayed almost entirely at the expense of the agency I worked for. But here in Recanati it didn't seem to work. I pulled out my lighter and moved on to my second move. Having moved the gas adjustment knob to the minimum, I could only get sparks and not ignite the flame. Again, this move did not have the desired effect. I was about to put the lighter away so I could finally smoke when someone approached me. It was my ex-husband. I gasped when I saw him.

«You cheating bastard, you still have the nerve to come near me?» I thought with my mind in turmoil and my heart already racing. I had the instinct to move away, without even looking at him, then I remembered what I had promised myself two years before, when I had caught him in bed with his lover. My heart calmed; my mind became clear. It was as if an alarm bell had gone off, an alarm clock had rung. He glanced at the dress I was wearing, red as passion, red as the blood I wanted to shed to satisfy my thirst for revenge.

«Do you still use these tricks to attract men to you?» he addressed me by lighting my cigarette.

«Paolo? What are you doing around here? Weren't you gone for good?» I questioned him, abandoning my thoughts, and staring at him with wild eyes.

«Well, I spent a couple of years in Milan for work. As you know, I had decided to become a writer. Embarking on such a career and achieving fame here in the Marche region would not have been possible, while in a big city you can always find good contacts».

«And did you find them?» I asked, with a hint of sarcasm.

«Yes, or at least I thought so. I let myself be duped by a writer-publisher; she made me believe that we would write a novel together, we would publish it, present it all over Italy, translate it into at least five foreign languages, that it would be an incredible launch on the market and that together we would earn hundreds of thousands, or rather, millions of Euros».

«She was getting you laid, wasn't she?» And I emphasized this question with a puff of smoke and a sidelong glance.

«Sure, and they were fabulous fucks. Then, when all was said and done, I wrote the novel almost in its entirety and she published it under her own name, liquidating me with a measly 10,000 Euro check».

«I guess now the book is at the top of the best-seller charts and you didn't even have the courage, I won't say to denounce her, but at least to publicly trash her».

«I didn't have any grounds to assert my rights. I had typed the manuscript in her house and on her computer. As long as it suited her, she kept me and maintained me; when the work was completed, a good kick in the ass and on to another».

«You men are incorrigible, you just need to see a skirt, a pair of legs or two nice breasts to lose your minds. But you in particular! And now what do you do? You come to seek refuge with your old companion, as if nothing had happened, thinking that time can erase even the worst wrongdoings?» Then, extinguishing the cigarette butt in the ashtray, I resumed. «Now I'll say goodbye, I have to go to work. At least you have spent a couple of years of your life in a big city, while I have continued to live in this country inhabited by gossipy and narrow-minded people. Leopardi was right about the Recanatesi: *Nor did my heart tell me I would be damned to spend my green age in this wild native village, among vile, ignorant people, whose strange names, often the subject of laughter and amusement, are doctrine and knowledge*».

With this poetic quotation, I left Paolo, giving him a provocative look, which was the prelude to what would happen in these hours. He looked at me as I moved away until I disappeared from his sight, I imagine convinced his ex-girlfriend had opened a door for him. At the moment, perhaps he saw me much more attractive and fascinating than when he lived with me. He had decided in his head he would come to see me that evening, convinced it would not be difficult to win me back. But yes, I would have left him believing that. At the end of the day, revenge is a dish that must be eaten cold, one cannot and should not leave room for haste and improvisation. Meanwhile, while waiting for the evening, I had to face a long day of work.

I worked all morning long, as there were still people booking their vacations, taking advantage of the low season and the more favorable prices. At noon, I asked the boss if I could leave a few minutes early, as I intended to stop by a real estate agency before it closed.

«You just got back from vacation today and you're already asking for favors?» Angelo, an opulent, white-haired sixty-year-old man, was the owner of the agency and used to stay holed up in his office, leaving his employees to deal with the public. Despite his reluctance, since the other girl had taken her vacation right after mine and he would therefore be left alone, he granted me permission, deciding in his heart there would be no harm in closing the store ten minutes earlier for that day.

Carla was almost my age; we had known each other since forever and for a period between us there had been a relationship that had gone beyond friendship, a lesbian relationship that went on for almost a year. Both of us disappointed by our men, we had discovered in homosexual relationships an unusual pleasure, which had almost resulted in morbidity, as we were searching for new emotions to be consumed in the intimacy of a bedroom. For a while, we had decided it was much better and more satisfying to make love between us than with a man, then we realized we were exceeding all limits and perhaps it was better to stop, if only to follow the common moral, which saw that relationship as perverse. I knew well that when Carla saw me, she still felt a strong urge towards me. I never wanted to give her strange ideas again, but that day I would have used her for my own purposes, so I had gone to talk to her. I walked the short distance separating me from the real estate agency, and I arrived there when my friend was about to close. Carla, a beautiful blonde with long wavy hair and hazel eyes, tiny but well-proportioned, gasped when she saw me coming and let me kiss her cheeks in greeting, while I carefully tried to avoid touching her lips.

«I would like to put my house up for sale», I told her with little preamble. «I want to leave this country; I've already got my eye on an apartment in the center of Ancona, not the best city, but better than here».

«I'll take this into consideration, even if it's not easy to sell in this period, the market is almost at a standstill», she replied, probably with her heart beating in her throat. «I should come to your house to take pictures, to put them in the catalog and display them in the window».

We remained staring into each other's eyes, a tear sprouted from her hazel eyes, to let my green eyes know that distance would have caused them grief. A hand, one of the four, reached for the key inserted in the lock of the inside of the window, gave a turn, after which two bodies found themselves embraced, wrapped in an uncontrollable desire. Clothes slid on the floor, naked bodies were hot, hands urgently sought them, lips found themselves glued together, breasts pressed against each other.

«My God, Manu! You can't do this to me, you can't abandon me. No, I don't want to have a relationship with you again, we decided together it was not the case. But it's enough for me to see you, to see you around town. Without you it will be like a light went out. Why, why did you come to me today? Do I have to be the one to sell your house? Why are you so cruel? Why?» Carla put on her clothes, nervous.

«Just do it. And stop whining», I replied, irritated by her behavior.

«*Damn nymphomaniac, you bastard too*», I brooded to myself. «*I've played your games all this time just to keep you in check. You're convinced that in the dark I didn't recognize you, but I know very well that it was you, that night, in my bed with my man. And now the time of reckoning has come*».

I remembered the scent well, all too well. The sheets were soaked in it, and I had smelled it even after having washed them in the washing machine at 70° C. A sweet fragrance, which I had then tracked down in the perfume shop; the saleswoman had explained that it was a niche perfume and only a few people liked it for its special scent. In the time we had been together, I had never noticed it on her.... But now... now I had no more doubts.

CHAPTER 2

Tuesday, green, anger

I woke up in the wrong mood. With my arm, I turned the alarm clock upside down when it rang, and I made it roll on the parquet floor. The ringing stopped and I stayed under the sheets for another five minutes. Then I pulled myself to my feet and quickly opened the organza curtains. The sun piercing the glass blinded me. My mood contrasted sharply with the beautiful day looming.

«It would take a thunderstorm and lots of rain», I thought.

I took a couple of things out of the closet without even looking at them and found a lilac tank top and a black mini skirt in my hand. I looked at the two pieces of clothing and then, huffing, I pulled them over the satin chair. I reopened the closet and spotted a fuchsia dress with thin straps. The hanger didn't come off the steel rod in the closet and, pulling hard, I broke the hook.

«That'll teach you to come off when I say so, you stupid hanger hook!» I hissed through my teeth.

I felt angry and agitated for bringing up the story of Carla and my husband, or rather my ex-husband. The anger was rising, like a river in flood, wanting to break its banks, to flood everything in its path.

I slipped under the lukewarm water of the shower, and I remembered all the times my body had given itself to Paolo's, and to Carla's. But then I was also imagining the bodies of the two adulterers, who had clutched each other in this very house, who perhaps had showered together under this very same jet. I was jealous of both. I took to vigorously scrubbing myself with the sponge until my skin turned purple. I wanted to erase the memories. I no longer wanted to feel Carla's hands caressing me under the gentle flow of the shower spray.

«Bitch!» I shouted into the stall and the voice bounced around the bathroom from wall to wall, until it came back to my ears as a prolonged echo. I hated her, and yet I still felt desire for her, so much so my hand couldn't help but slide down to my lower belly, just from calling to mind her image, the image of her wonderful naked body. No, I should not give in to an insulting feeling, which now had nothing real and tangible. I moved my hand firmly away from my private parts, turned off the tap and looked for my bathrobe, put it on, quickly rubbed my body and then dwelt on the color of the terrycloth garment. Green, the color of anger. This would be the day of rage, so the clothing had to match that color. I went back to my room and abandoned the idea of lilac and fuchsia clothes, which would have been more appropriate for a fifteen-year-old girl on her first date. I wore a knee-length skirt with a plaid check pattern, in which green was the predominant color, and dressed my legs in a light pantyhose of the same color. I chose a lace bra, over which I went to arrange a twin set also green, short-sleeved shirt and cotton sweater. I sprayed my hair with hairspray that gave it a greenish sheen and chose earrings with a small emerald stone pendant. Final touch: green leather handbag and python shoes. Even the pack of cigarettes I went to put in my bag was that color. I had found it in a particular tobacco shop, which sold all those fancy packets. On it the writing read "Chiaravalle", 100% Virginia Tobacco without additives. The name came from the fact they were produced in the factory of the so named small town in the Marche region of Italy, but I, Emanuela "La Capricciosa", cared little about all that; what was important was the bright green color of the packet. A generous spritz of perfume, of *that* perfume, and I was ready to go out.

The day had been hot since early morning, and I had dressed heavy for the season, but who cared? I felt very sexy, irresistible, and this would help me to better organize my revenge. The anger I felt inside could have been a bad counselor, even instigating me to kill. But the rationality in me always prevailed over all other impulses and feelings. What is the point of killing, after all? It's an end in itself, it quenches your thirst for revenge for a short time and then, if you manage not to get caught by the police and end up in jail for life, your satisfaction will be relegated to a remote corner of your mind, of your brain, until it falls into oblivion. Organizing a revenge that comes to discredit forever the person - or people - object of your contempt, has much more value. Just think of the satisfaction of seeing that person turn his head down for the rest of their life. You can point your gaze at him, watching him blushing and turning away. That was what I would do, and I would succeed.

That morning, without even having to make a big scene, Paolo came over to my table and lit my cigarette. I, almost as if it were a foregone conclusion, took his hands between mine to bring the flame of the lighter closer. I understood he was not insensitive to the gesture. My hands had brushed against his as if in a tender caress. All studied, all premeditated. There was seduction in the gesture, but in the depths of my eyes I could glimpse a hint of malice, which perhaps did not escape Paolo.

«Oh no, Manu! You're so...sexy, so...desirable. Yet there's something about you, a shadow that's almost awe-inspiring right now», he murmured with some embarrassment.

I grabbed him by the collar of his shirt, drew him to me, and puffed cigarette smoke in his face. My instinct was to deliver a good kick under the coffee table with the toe of my shoe, directly to his testicles, but I restrained myself. I smiled sardonically at him and tried a lunge.

«Is your cell phone number still the same?»

«Yes, why?» he replied, readjusting his shirt, and lighting a cigarette perhaps more out of disengagement than a desire to smoke. «Are you maybe going to invite me to your house one of these evenings?»

«You never know. Would you come?»

«That depends. An intimate dinner just you and me?»

«Maybe yes, maybe no. Maybe a dinner yes, but maybe there will be other guests. I'll let you know», and I left him in the grip of curiosity, getting up from the bar table. My skirt had risen to mid-thigh hinting at my ill-concealed availability to him. I was pleased with myself about the way I had baited him. I lowered the hem of my skirt with my hands and waddled back to my office.

Fortunately, few people came into the agency that day. I talked a fifty-something couple out of booking a ten-day cruise in the Mediterranean, giving the shipping company some well-deserved bad publicity. I sent a distinguished gentleman, who wanted to take a relaxing vacation in a quiet hotel in the Dolomites, to another travel agency, stating we liked to send our clients to much more eventful places and we didn't deal with the target audience he required. Halfway through the morning I felt it was getting hot, and clearly Angelo, to save money, had purposely not turned on the air conditioning. I slipped off my cotton sweater, remaining with the bright half-sleeved shirt. I took my cigarettes and lighter and went to smoke outside, taking a look at my fellow citizens who pretended to be busy to the nth degree, walking along Corso Persiani at a good pace to reach a bank, or the post office, with the ultimate aim of having a chat and say bad things about that and that other, waiting for their turn and hoping that the employee was as usual slow enough to allow free rein to the right gossip of the country.

I took my last puff of smoke, threw away the cigarette butt and went back inside, earning the air conditioning remote control and turning it on, amidst the almost incomprehensible protests and mutterings of my employer. If I'd had a knife handy, I would have plunged it into his chest, straight into his heart. But the best you could find in that office was a letter opener, not even a sharp one to be honest, so much so it had been a while since anyone had used it to open the mail, at most it could remove the dirt under the nails.

«This is a quiet time», he told me, looking at me sideways. «If you want, you can take your weekly half-day off this afternoon. Even if Lorella isn't here, I'll take care of things here».

I gladly accepted and thanked him, even though I knew she had suggested having noticed my bad mood and considering how I had treated the only customers of the morning. If it weren't for being inept and that I was practically the one who kept the business going for a meager salary and some commission, she would have treated me differently. But it was in her interest to keep me happy; I knew it, and sometimes I took advantage of it.

Since there were no customers, now that the air conditioning was on and there was still more than an hour to go before closing time, I took the opportunity to surf the Internet. I wanted the latest news about Paolo, because I didn't trust what he had told me about his ménage with the writer from Milan. I typed "Paolo Biondi" in the Google bar and scrolled through the search results. I was struck in particular by a literary blog that reported an interview with him released some time before to a journalist - literary critic. The headline: "After separating from the beautiful Aurora Centofanti, writer Paolo Biondi starts anew". It was getting interesting. I opened the article page and read carefully. I peeked toward the back office to make sure the boss wasn't spying on what I was doing. Angelo was reading the pink newspaper, the classic sports paper, smoking his cigar and turning his back. Well, if he was smoking, it was all right for me to smoke as well. I put a cigarette between my lips, and continued to keep it in my mouth unlit, fiddling with the lighter and concentrating on what I was reading. At the end I sent the article to the printer, retrieved the paper, and finally lit the cigarette. I was so nervous and irritated by what I had read I unfortunately I brought the flame of the still-lit lighter close to a lock of hair, which sizzled and gave off a foul burning smell. No harm done, that same evening I would have gone to the hairdresser to have my hair done. Maybe I would have had my hair dyed, I would have changed the color of my hair, I would have gone blonde, why not? To indicate a change, a turning point in my life. But that remained to be seen, I would think about it in due time.

Back home, I realized my stomach was in knots, I took a bite of a sandwich and felt nauseated; I had a spasm, almost a gag reflex. I picked up the paper I had printed at the office, I read and reread it, until I had almost memorized every single word, smoking one cigarette after another until I finished the packet. My heart was filled with anger as the room was saturated with smoke. I felt hot, very hot. I stripped, naked, and stretched out on the couch in the living room. The thought of Paolo in the arms of that nymphomaniac Carla, then again in the perverse relationship with the woman from Milan, a relationship from which he had taken the ideas for the forthcoming novel, on the one hand made me angry, on the other excited me. I felt my lower abdomen pulsate, then wet with a slight trickle of liquid. I couldn't help myself. I was sweating, I wanted to light a cigarette to calm down, but there were no more, and so I gave free rein to my body, to my instincts, until, after several minutes, I reached the peak of my excitement. I arched my back, then relaxed and fell deeply asleep. And I dreamed.

There was a rainbow in the sky, the white light was refracted by endless tiny water droplets suspended in the air, in the seven colors of the iris. At its base, matching each color, seven victims awaited their execution. Some were tied to a pole on top of a pile of wood, some had their heads resting on a stump, some, blindfolded, were waiting for the discharge of bullets that would fall on them, some were ready to receive a lethal injection, and others the deadly electric discharge. Compared to the beginning of the dream, in which those characters were undefined and had no face, now I could recognize one by one those silhouettes, people who had somehow had relations with me, people who had somehow betrayed me. With a large axe, I had approached the victim next to the red. It was Paolo: "Commend your soul to the Lord, if you believe there is someone worthy to receive you into the kingdom of the dead". The head had rolled away, the blood had splashed forcefully toward me, but the victim's eyes continued to stare at me with a still vital gaze.

I woke up in a bath of sweat, realizing that someone was insistently ringing the doorbell. I slipped on a red robe, hastily retrieved from somewhere, over my naked body and glanced at the clock, it was six o'clock in the afternoon. I approached the entrance and asked from behind the door who it was, almost shouting.

«I'm Carla. I came to take pictures of your property....»

I opened the door reluctantly; the photos were an excuse. Carla came in with a lit cigarette and the digital camera in her hand, threw the packet and lighter on the living room table and threw herself on an armchair. I took advantage of the cigarettes, lighting one and sat down on the same couch where I had slept a short time before. I crossed my bare legs, while my robe, on the front, barely covered my nakedness.

«Is this how you show up, Carla? The house is in total disorder, you should have at least warned me that you were coming. But I think the reason for your visit is another, you're spying on me, trying to find out if I have other relationships. Well, know that, as I told you clearly yesterday, everything is over between us, I am completely free».

Not minding my words, the other attacked me.

«It was here, wasn't it? You've spent hours together. I know, I can still smell in the air the sex that took place here».

«Who are you referring to?»

«Come on, don't play dumb! They saw you yesterday, having breakfast at the bar with Paolo, in Piazza Leopardi. Wasn't what he put you through in the past enough? All men are the same, liars, mean, traitors. Much better to be among us women», and so saying she unbuttoned her blouse, opening it wide, showing off her breasts and trying simultaneously to straddle my legs.

«What are you doing?» I said in resentment, standing up abruptly and shaking her off. «That's enough. I've decided right now not to sell this house again, and if I ever have second thoughts I'll go to another agency. And now go away, please».

Carla recomposed herself, perhaps realizing that she had gone too far, rearranged her clothes and took one last look at one of my breast, which in the confusion had remained uncovered, then walked out the door without another word.

«But we shall see each other again! Oh yes, we'll see each other again, my dear Manu!» I heard her brooding to herself.

Irritated by the situation, I violently put out my cigarette butt in the ashtray, then headed for the bathroom to freshen up. I only took a few steps when the doorbell rang again. I opened the door: «Carla, I told you to go...» Without even having time to finish the sentence, I felt myself wrapped in a violent embrace; it was useless to resist, I felt my robe ripped off, I lost my balance and fell with my bare back on the cold floor. As soon as I touched the ground, I found Carla's body, with all its weight, on top of me. My instinct was to react violently, to smack her in the face. But I remained motionless. The closeness of her face, her blond hair falling to brush against my cheeks, brought back to my mind the image of the dream. She was the witch, the woman tied to the stake awaiting execution on top of a huge pile of wood. And yes, the Church, until a few centuries ago, put homosexuals with witches and heretics, and many had ended up at the stake. I was already pondering how I could set her on fire for real, but the lighter I had would have been just enough to barely burn her. But once again I went back my homicidal instinct and, even giving in a little to the pleasure I got from her closeness and her insistence on touching me, I reasoned. As I panted, letting Carla run her hands over my body, over my nipples, over my clitoris especially, my mind opened, my plans became more and more lucid. Yes... Yes... Yes... She, Carla, she would be the main pawn in my revenge against Paolo. Ah... Ah... Ahhhhhh... I felt the nymphomaniac's body sag over me. She had climaxed and was now fulfilled. And so was I, probably, and even the anger I had been pervaded by all day had sort of dissipated in that moment. I felt light, even though

Carla's body still lay abandoned on top of me. And I knew what I had to do over the next few days.

CHAPTER 3

Wednesday, Fuchsia, gluttony

I was tired! I lifted my arms upward and stretched in my office chair. I stood up and leaned forward. I stood like this for a few seconds, silent and still. It was nice to feel my spine relax as the strands of hair reached down to tickle my legs. The hairdresser had done a good job. Having failed to do so the day before, I had made an appointment to see him early in the morning. He had suggested highlights, and I agreed, but with streaked locks in fuchsia pink, which would have gone perfectly with that day's outfit, a short dress, a light pantyhose - 8 DEN pastel summer tights - makeup and lipstick in the same color shades.

When I straighten up, my hair slid over my shoulders, puffy and neat. I sensed a few rumblings in my stomach. I was hungry, but not for a plate of spaghetti, or a steak, or even pizza. My mind wandered back thinking about the inviting and delicious pastries made by Mrs. Maria, the owner of the pastry shop in Piazzetta Sant'Agostino, not far from where I was at that moment.

I adjusted the hem of my tight-fitting dress which, while sitting, had risen beyond all limits of decency, fixed my hair with the tips of my fingers, slipped my feet into my 12-heeled pumps, which had been left under the desk for some time, and left the office.

I walked the short stretch of road in the shadow of the old buildings in the center. I passed in front of the sports bar and a whistle of approval came from some boys in the group standing there. I had to smile: men! They have only to see a beautiful woman and they immediately lose their heads, even looking foolish, with no shame, with no restraint, especially in a small provincial town, where there is not much to do.

When I finally arrived at my destination, Mrs. Maria was not there; in her place was her unpleasant daughter, tall as a cuirassier and just as fat and un-gainly. She looked at me from head to toe, lingering a little longer on my legs, long and well-shaped, per-haps with a hint of envy in her gaze.

«I'd like a tray of cream puffs», I began, shifting my enchanted gaze to the small mignons behind the glass window.

I saw her out of the corner of my eye pick up a pink cardboard tray and, with tongs in hand, wait silently for me to decide what to take.

«Put in three cream puffs and two hazelnut puffs, then the brioche with mascarpone and Nutella and to finish...» I told her, pausing for a moment to choose the last treat. «Also, a couple of those pastries with strawberry».

The girl was about to wrap the tray when I stopped her.

«I'll eat some at the small table out there; I'm really craving sweets today. I don't get fat anyway!» and I deliberately emphasized the last words.

The girl, in front of me, did not blink and I, smiling at her, sat down outside. I began with the cream puffs. My favorite, with a soft texture inside and tough outside: they melted in my mouth. . I closed my eyes as I was tasting these delicious treats and the games my ex husband and I sometimes played in bed with Mrs. Maria's pastries came back to me. I caught myself remembering the time when he and I spread the cream, cold from the refrigerator on each other, then savored it with our tongues, our lips burning with desire. A shiver of pleasure ran down my spine. Maybe the memory was still very present, or at least more present than I thought. Those had been good times, seductive and imaginative, before Paolo started playing with other women, as well as with me.

I drank a glass of fresh water and turned my attention to the pastry filled with pieces of strawberries and wisps of cream. It was simply delicious and inviting. We had also played with strawberries and cream, and I had eaten so many, scattered over Paolo's body, that I had woken up with hives the next morning.

I felt like laughing.

I also ate the hazelnut cream puffs, I put them one at a time, completely in my mouth, like a greedy child. I tasted them, feeling the flavor in my nostrils. This reminded me of the evening of one birthday, when Paolo had prepared a meringue cake with cream and chocolate, which was also tasted in an unconventional way.

The brioche, the only one left, was eyeing me from the tray; overflowing with mascarpone cheese with thick lines of Nutella intertwined divinely with each other. But before I tackled her, I took out of my purse the crumpled sheet of paper I had printed the day before and laid it on the table to read it for the umpteenth time. At that moment perhaps, with a stomach full to the point of nausea, I could have faced the reading more relaxed. We all know that sweet food favors the release of endorphins, promoting relaxation and easing tensions, both physical and psychic. Yes, now those are the emotions I felt, still desire for revenge, but the anger had calmed down; now it was necessary to organize everything calmly.

Q - Critics say that your new novel will be a best-seller. Is it true that for the most salacious descriptions you have been inspired by the sexual relations you had with your former partner, Centofanti?

A - I don't want to anticipate anything. All I'm saying is that our relationship was... spicy, not innocent. And every writer takes his or her cue from real, lived situations. All I'm saying is that the title of the novel will be very intriguing.

Q - Not a romance novel, as expected from the collaboration of two writers like yourselves, but a "hard", erotic novel, which will be published under your sole signature. How did our Aurora take this? Sales in the order of a million copies, translation and circulation abroad are expected. Do you foresee any legal battles from your former partner?

A - I don't want to predict anything and I don't want to give away what she is saying. All I can say is that the manuscript is on the table of the main Italian publishing houses; we will see which one will make the most attractive proposal.

Q - They say that a well-known director wants to make a film out of your novel, and that the role of the male in-

terpreter, who would represent you, Paolo Biondi, has even been proposed to Rocco Siffredi. Great returns are expected, then. Your royalties will be considerable this time. Is this true?

A - I know nothing about it yet. As I repeat, I do not want to make any advance comments.

Q - At least answer us on one fact. Is it true that you want to go into politics? We know from reliable sources that you will return to the Marche region to stand in the next elections as Governor of your home region.

A - This is true. I was contacted by the Innovation Party, and I accepted the candidacy.

And that was the interesting news, the pivot of my revenge. Paolo would go into politics; he had come back to Recanati for that. And a politician is a public figure, a person in the public eye, constantly under the watchful eye of his constituents, someone who, if caught red-handed doing things outside of common morality, even if in private, stakes his career and reputation overnight.

The time had come to call in and bring another pawn into play, Carla's former partner, Tonino. I had known him since high school, one year we had even been classmates and I had noticed a certain interest in him towards me, an interest never reciprocated. After high school, he then got engaged and married to Carla, unfortunately realizing at his own expense that the latter was very prone to betrayal. Yes, that had enraged him. One evening, having returned home earlier than usual, he had surprised his wife in bed with her lover. The two, focused on intercourse, hadn't even noticed he had entered, so he had gone into the kitchen and armed himself with the longest and sharpest knife there was. Tonino was strong, and had caught his rival by surprise, grabbing him with an arm around the neck, pulling him up from the bed and threatening to emasculate him. He had brought the knife close to his still erect member, when the other, with a desperate move, had escaped his grasp and had thrown himself out of the window, naked as he was. The room was only on the second floor; the guy despite having sprained his ankle, and limping a little, had disappeared in the dark. Tonino had no choice but to take it out on his wife, Carla, who was still on the bed, naked, in all her dazzling beauty. He had pounced on her, straddled her belly, and raised the knife, gripping it with both hands. He would have sunk it into her chest, right between her breasts, if his gaze hadn't met her eyes, not at all intimidated. The eyes of an eager cat, claiming sex, claiming that someone, no matter who, would finish what had been left unfinished a short time before. Tonino, abandoned his weapon, had possessed her body for the last time, with rage, with violence, with contempt, with no loving or even affectionate impulse. In that embrace he had unloaded all his hatred towards Carla; only the ejaculation had appeased his anger. He would have wanted to slap her, before leaving, but he didn't. He left her yet panting, he didn't even take his things and left that place forever. So Recanati was a distant memory for Inspector Tonino Della Valle, on duty at the Torino Porta Nuova police district. That was a fact. He had run away from Recanati like a coward, enlisting in the police force in a big city like Turin, which had allowed him to live his life as one of the many, without having to account for his actions to anyone, without fear of being caught up in the village gossip, without having to constantly check on those who looked at him from behind in the street, while in their thoughts mocking him for having been cheated on more than once by his wife.

Now I had to take advantage of his being a career cop, an inspector, probably waiting for his promotion to commissioner. Hoping that he hadn't changed his cell phone number, I looked up his name in the phone book and initiated the call. I counted many empty rings, imagining the scene on the other end, him sitting at a desk, barricaded behind a mountain of paperwork, looking puzzled on the display at the name of the caller - Emanuela - undecided whether to answer or not. I was about to give up when I heard his voice.

«Inspector Tonino Della Valle», he answered as if he didn't know who was calling him.

«Tonino, it's Emanuela, you remember me, don't you?» I said after a few moments of embarrassed silence, in an uncertain voice, as if searching for the right words. A smart policeman would certainly have understood that I was preparing to bluff, to tell a bunch of lies, but Tonino followed his own direction.

«I recognize you, unfortunately, and to be honest, I don't really appreciate your call. I've broken my ties with Recanati and I'm happy about that. If you are then going to tell me about Carla, we can hang up immediately. Thanks for the thought and thanks for listening to me. Forget that old Tonino still exists, just as you have done so far».

«Please don't talk like that, your ex-wife....»

«Carla is not my ex, by law we are still married. I have had her lawyer write to her several times, but she has never shown up for her separation hearings», he replied in an irritated tone. Fearing he would hang up, I quickly tried to cut to the chase.

«It's not Carla I wanted to talk to you about. That is, even about her. But mostly about me, and about Paolo, who has returned to Recanati. The two lovebirds may get back together again».

«So what? Would you like me to come back too, to organize with you a cross revenge against the two lovers, a nice double murder, perhaps using my service pistol? Or, more simply, do you think I should take the opportunity to finally get a divorce? I told you, I'm fine where I am and have no intention of moving».

«And yet, thanks to me, you might have the chance to make a name for yourself as a brilliant policeman, put yourself in the spotlight in front of your superiors, finally be promoted to the rank of commissioner and - why not? - move closer to your places of origin».

«Oh, really! Should I do my police exploits right outside my jurisdiction? And how would I justify it? And then why, please tell me, should I reconnect with my places of origin if that is not what I want?»

«Because perhaps there is someone who still thinks of you. You see, I've never confessed this to you, but I've been secretly in love with you since high school». I heard him sigh and become speechless. I let a few moments of silence pass, basking in the satisfaction of having him in my grasp, then resumed, «We don't need to talk about this now over the phone. I'll send you an e-mail explaining how you can arrest Paolo and Carla. You'll see, you won't be able to refuse. The game is too intriguing».

I closed the connection, certain that leaving him at the mercy of curiosity would work in my favor. The last person who had to be present in Recanati to close the circle was Aurora Centofanti. Difficult, but not impossible, drawing her into my web.

CHAPTER 4

Thursday, indigo, pride

Indigo is an unusual color, a shade that in the spectrum of the iris is between blue and violet. It is the color tinging the sky at dawn or at dusk, in the transition from night to day, or vice versa. Somewhere I had read each person gives off an aura of a different color depending on the person's personality or mood. An indigo aura is usually associated with an arrogant person in an evil mood. That was the color that suited the day about to begin. Before I even got out of bed, I lit a cigarette, opened my underwear drawer in the half-light and carefully selected my accessories, bra, panties, guepiere and black stockings. Then I peeked into the closet, from which I took a white silk blouse with half sleeves, a turquoise skirt, and a matching jacket. I left the collar of the blouse unbuttoned so my décolletage would be well visible. I reached the bathroom, where the cigarette butt went out when it came in contact with the water in the toilet bowl. I flushed the toilet and carefully applied my makeup. My pride suggested at that moment I was looking in the mirror at the most beautiful woman in the world. I could have had both men and women under my feet. I imagined the scene: Carla and Aurora under the heels of my shoes, one on each side, submissive like two mangy dogs, while with my hands I held Paolo and Tonino on a leash, obedient to my every will. I omnipotent could have reserved life or death for my succubus demons at my pleasure. Too bad I couldn't actually experience the scene. I went to the kitchen and, instead of putting on the coffee, searched the bottom of a drawer. I needed to get myself ready for that day. The white powder was still there, who knows how long. I had promised myself not to use it anymore from one night I had abused it with Carla. She made me try it. I didn't want to, but then I had a taste for it. At the moment there was enough coca to make three lines. I prepared them on the kitchen table, then, helping myself with a rolled up ten-euro bill, I sucked deeply the first one. I felt my nose burning, my head exploding. I snorted the second line. Before tackling the third, I drank a glass of water, lit a cigarette, took a couple of puffs, left it smoking in the ashtray, then inhaled again, this time much more calmly. Now I could face the day, considering myself not only the most beautiful woman in the world, but also the strongest, the invincible, the indestructible. *"Tremble in fear, people! Emanuela La Capricciosa is about to hit the streets"*. I grabbed my cell phone and searched the address book for a particular name: Delirium. I let it ring twice, closed the line, and waited for him to call me back.

«Do you have any parties in the works, Manuela? I've got some great "stuff" this week, directly from Albania. A little expensive, but of excellent quality. Come see me tonight, from seven o'clock on, at the usual bar».

«Saturday night will be a reunion with friends, so I spare no expense. Make me a dozen gift packages and I'll give you twice as much as you ask of other customers. As long as it's really good quality, otherwise....»

«Otherwise, what are you going to do, mate with me? I can't wait!»

«Don't be an asshole. I have friends on the force, and certainly a visit from them might not be appreciated. I'll see you tonight».

I walked out into the street with my vision a little blurry. The day was beautiful. I breathed in the fresh morning air at the top of my lungs and regained my lucidity. To be one hundred percent on point, I decided not to order the usual cappuccino with brioche, but rather to have a double coffee, accompanied by a glass of sparkling water.

The waiter, a young man of about twenty, looked at me smugly and did not spare a joke.

«Gee, Manu, judging by your appearance you must have had quite a busy night!»

I didn't even answer him, but to provoke him I crossed my legs, so the skirt lifted to highlight the hem of my stockings, garters and even panties. Then I dropped the container with the paper towels on the floor, right next to my feet. I wanted to see if the young man had taken advantage of the opportunity to bring his eyes close to my body, but he pretended not to notice, blushed a little and disappeared into the bar to fill mine and other orders.

While I waited for the waiter to return, I rummaged through my purse in desperate search of a package that wasn't there. Wow, in the euphoria of the "sniff", I had forgotten it on the kitchen table. No big deal, I would have gone to the tobacco shop before reaching the office. But at that moment? How could I satisfy the need to take nicotine and still have in my hands an object of the baggage of my seductive arts? That morning, the inevitable Paolo did not show up to offer me a cigarette. Was he late or was I early? Who appeared instead was Leonardo Gerbilli, the photographer of the Gerbilli and Lomonaco agency, which had its headquarters a short distance from the travel agency.

«So, Emanuela? What do you have so appealing to offer me? Unexpected earnings, you promised me on the phone, but even if it weren't money and it was your personal compensation, it would still be fine with me. You're still a gorgeous woman!»

The guy was holding out the open pack of cigarettes toward me, waiting for me to take one. It had completely slipped my mind I had called him the night before.

«I still don't quite understand what your agency deals with, whether you're a private detective agency, or gossip-type scoop seekers, but I do know when you have *hot* photos on your hands you charge a lot for them. Or you sell them at a high price to those who should not have been portrayed in them, or to the other party if they offer more, or to some newspaper if it is suitable material and can be well paid. In short, what I figured out about you is you're a despicable human being!» I said, slipping a cigarette from his pack and allowing him to light it for me. «But this time you won't have to do anything. I'll be the one to provide you with the material. And top-shape materials, you'll see. And I won't even want any compensation for the favor I'm doing you. I'll just have the satisfaction of knowing some people will be fucked up for life!»

«Prominent people, Manu?»

«Very prominent, Leo, very prominent. People of national, maybe international fame. And you, thanks to the material I will provide, will be able to turn them into dust».

I looked at him languidly. He brought his face closer to my ear, I felt his breath and the good aroma of his aftershave close.

«Don't you want to give me anything in advance?» he whispered, brushing my cheek with his lips. I turned mine to his, to make him believe I wanted him to kiss me, but instead I suddenly puffed smoke at him, causing him to pull away a little.

«I want to keep you curious, although you only have to read a few local newspapers to know who has returned here to Recanati after a long absence», and I winked at him. He remained silent and lit a cigarette too without taking his gaze off my eyes for a moment, letting me know he understood perfectly who we were talking about.

«Manu, Manu! You have two beautiful eyes, but they manage to conceal very little of what lies behind them. Take it from someone who knows».

«Play it cool and remember what I'm telling you. You'll have your material Sunday night. Be at the Hotel Dorico in Ancona at four o'clock in the afternoon. Here's the card with the address. You will ask for a reserved room, where some people are waiting for you to play Poker».

«So, you have gambling in mind. What kind? Poker?»

«No, my dear: Strip-Poker. He who stays in his underwear, loses!» and I dismissed him with a mischievous smile. He too was now part of the game, and he was one of the most important pawns. I had been getting my house ready for some time, and I had spared no expense. The important thing was to get the final revenge. I knew that sooner or later the time would come. Every now and then I pulled aside the heavy curtain in the living room That hid the security door, which was not a safe, but it gave access to the secret part of my home. That day, back home for lunch, I hesitated in front of the security door, then, as if driven by an external will, almost not mine, I typed the combination on the keypad and clicked the lock. I went down the stairs and sniffed with pleasure the smell of new plaster and fresh paint that emanated from the room. Eight rooms, each a different color, one red, one orange, one yellow, one part green part blue, one indigo, one purple. Then there was a white room and a black room. In each room there was a bed in the center, on the walls a few indispensable furnishings. Only the blue and green room had a double bed.

White and black are perceived by our eye, but they are not real colors. The first comes by the fusion of the other seven colors of the iris. At the bottom of the stairs, I found myself in the white room, where there was no bed, but an enamel table above which was the beating heart of the whole room, a small but powerful McIntosh, from which, through a system of sophisticated cameras, it was possible to control every single room. The same computer controlled the opening or closing of every door. There were two doors in each wall of the room, except in the one you accessed from the room above. Each door gave access to one of the colorful rooms.

Black is not a color. While a white object reflects the radiations of the whole visible range, a black one absorbs them all, swallows them giving nothing back, like a black hole at the center of a galaxy swallows matter purging it in another dimension unknown to us. The black room was empty and dark. You could enter on it only through each of the other rooms. There was no direct access from the white room, like for all the other rooms.

I lifted the lid of the computer, connected to the Internet in anonymously way. A scale map of the room appeared on the screen, and I controlled the opening of the red door with the mouse. A small click, and the new environment was accessible. Excited, I approached, pushed open the door and entered the room illuminated by a soft light. Touching them with the palm of my hand, the vermilion sheets gave me the sensation of a shiver. It ran down my back, reaching my most intimate parts, which throbbed at the mere thought of what it would happen there in the coming hours and days.

I closed everything up, hesitating to enjoy the new and clean smell again, and went up the stairs to the living room. The time had come to throw out the bait and attract the first victim. Emanuela "La Superba" dialed the number of Paolo "Il Succubo" on her cell phone.

«Tonight, I don't feel like being alone», I attacked in the most persuasive voice I was capable of. «Would you like to come over for dinner?»

Paolo's eyes had certainly adjusted to the dimness of the room. I shone the flame of the lighter to illuminate my face. I had placed the ashtray on my naked body, just above my belly button. The tip of the cigarette glowed red with every puff. Red was the color that had dominated the evening: red the walls of the bedroom, red the nightgown I was wearing, before he took it off revealing that even the underwear, bra, panties, guepiere and stockings were that color. Mine was a terraced house with a red brick facade in the "Le Grazie" district, on the sloping part of the hill facing the Marche hinterland. He had arrived there at the dusk. I had caught a glimpse of him, from behind the curtains, while he was looking at the silhouettes of the mountains standing out against the red sky. He hesitated for a moment before ringing the doorbell, then he had found the courage and had not regretted it. I imagine that in the soft light of the sunset, dressed in the same colors that nature was offering at that moment, he saw me even more beautiful than ever. I had carefully prepared a dinner for two, in which every dish recalled the color red: thin noodles with shrimp sauce, lobster, radicchio, and a delicious dessert enriched with raspberries and blueberries. Against all rules, I had also put red wine on the table. At the end of the meal, I had taken Paolo by the hand, I had drawn him to me without saying a word, I had kissed him for a long time and, without him even realizing it, I had taken him down to the red room, disappearing for a few minutes and coming back ready to make love. He made me undress him, then he had taken off my nightgown. Lying on the bed, one next to the other, we had kissed and caressed each other for a long time, then, one after the other, the accessories of my clothing had been removed. I had made sure that only my stockings remained on, to make Paolo feel even more pleasure in passing his hand to touch their silky nylon. After the first embrace, I had those slipped off, gently, with no hurry, and then he had made love again until he reached orgasm.

At the end I had tried to grab the package and the ashtray on the bedside table. He, seeing me smoke, felt like doing the same. It was what I had been waiting for. I had just gotten the goods from Delirium before going home. I had prepared cigarettes in which the tobacco had been mixed with a particular drug, which would have dulled Paolo's senses and subjected him to my will. I pretended to fall asleep, while I peeked at Paolo taking distracted puffs of smoke and looking at me with a mixture of satisfaction and jealousy. I think he had never made love to me in such an intense way all over his life. In that moment he certainly thought *his* woman, after he left her, had practiced other men.

"How many men will she have taken into her bed? One a night? Maybe more than one at a time?" I

think he was imagining unbelievable orgies, not even realizing a throbbing tension headache was tightening its grip. I opened my eyes to enjoy the scene. Paolo's gaze was lost, he appeared like a person who sees the room turning, whirling around more and more. I took him by the hand and led him to a cooler, darker, pitch-black place. My words were muffled and distorted to his ears: «Come, we will make love as I say, in the place you deserve».

"Revenge... The time has come... You are the first victim... But then it will be someone else's turn..." I was saying to myself.

Of course, I wasn't exactly lucid either. After all, I had had my fair share of drugs and alcohol during the day. Leaving Paolo behind, I climbed the stairs, closed the security door, and reached my bedroom, lying completely naked, without even covering myself with a sheet.

Again, I was captured by dreamlike visions. I don't even know if in that moment I was sleeping or not, but I relived the scene in which I had surprised Paolo, right in that bed where I was lying, with Carla, in the half-light of the room. The way I relived that scene was garbled, as if in that moment I was doing what I had wanted to do at the time and had not had the courage to do. *"The cigarettes, where are the cigarettes? Ah, here they are!"*

I had a box of big fireplace matches in my hand. I lit one and kept looking at the lit match until I burned my fingers. Suicide, why not? By fire, of course, by fire. By this time, the cheaters had now disappeared. I approached the bed and, lighting one match after another, I set it on fire. There was nothing left to do but to lie down on that bed of seduction, betrayal, death, and let myself be captured by a warm, last, burning embrace. And to abandon myself to one last desired embrace, masturbating just in the moment I was going from life to death. So, while the stake waited ardently for me to offer myself to the extreme sacrifice, a flame grabbed a hem of my red dress. It danced, first yellowish, then red. Suddenly, an idea flashed in my mind, looking at those colors. With the palm of my hand, I smothered the flame, moved away, went outside, and watched my apartment burning. The flames rose, the smoke changed color depending on what it was ravishing, now white, now gray, now black. The colors, the colors of the iris, seven colors, seven like the days of the week, seven like the deadly sins, seven like the rooms I would prepare for my revenge to be carried out.

I awoke in the usual sweat bath, conscious that I had never set fire to my bed, but aware the actions that would lead to the satisfaction of my thirst for revenge had begun, and would end in the best way, the one I had always dreamed of.

CHAPTER 5

Friday, orange, greed

Orange is a strange, peculiar color, softer than red, but brighter than yellow. This was the color of that day, a color that immediately made me think of a 50 Euro bill. As I was getting dressed, I associated the thought of money with another of the seven deadly sins: avarice. But avarice is not only wanting to accumulate money and worldly goods, I thought, it is also wanting to keep something for yourself without sharing it with others. And my mind wondered to Aurora Centofanti, penetrating itself into her unaware brain and seizing information that, with a minimum intuition, anyone could have grabbed. Meanwhile, I was looking through my wardrobe for clothes and accessories in an impossible orange color: a dress with round sleeves and a pleated skirt that came close to the knee, a pantyhose in shades of orange, the same heaviness as a leotard, but which I put on anyway despite the season, "wedge" shoes in the same color bought who knows when, and never worn in my life, a shawl in bright colors to cover the wide back neckline. And then the makeup, which had to be in the same color. I even found a bag to match. And the cigarettes? I remembered having somewhere a pack of orange KIMs, the first brand of cigarettes I had bought as a girl. It was a brand discontinued for years and I had wanted to keep it as a nostalgic memory of. I rummaged to the bottom of a drawer and found it. I lit one. I remembered they had a poor scent, which probably, because of the aging of the tobacco, had almost disappeared, but it did not matter; what was important was the color of the package.

Before leaving the house, I had to retrieve Paolo's Smartphone. It was well in view on the coffee table in the living room. I scrolled through the address book and found the name I was looking for, Aurora Centofanti, the person whose sense of avarice I wanted to arouse and bring to the maximum. Touching the touch screen with a finger, I initiated the call. A rather irritated female voice answered, perhaps because of the time of the morning at which she was being disturbed, but more likely because of the name she had seen appearing on the display.

«It takes a lot of nerve to call me, Pa...»

I had to be quick to make her understand the call wasn't coming from Paolo, but from a woman with something to offer her.

«Don't worry», I told her in a persuasive voice. «I'm not Paolo, I'm his ex-wife and I have some interesting things to tell you, if you'd like to listen».

«Oh, really! Should I listen to you? Has the lost sheep returned to the pen? Well, you can keep him, I don't know what to do with him anymore!»

«Listen to me and you won't regret it. Yes, Paul came here, but don't think I want to forgive him; on the contrary, I want to take revenge on him, on his betrayals, and we can help each other. I imagine you also have resentments. You see, I know that Paolo has sent the manuscript of his new novel to important publishing houses, who are evaluating it. It seems it could become a best seller, it seems there might become a movie, in short, it seems there will be good money to be made from this work. But I also know that it's not all his own work».

«Nice find! The pig cheated me. We wrote a novel based on our life and our sex experiences. He wrote the spicy parts, but the plot, the real one, the one giving substance to the story, I wrote that. When the work was done, he downloaded the file onto his flash drive and deleted it permanently from my PC. So, I don't even have a chance to assert my rights. And everyone will know what we did in bed together, all over Italy, and maybe even half of Europe».

«But this time we can fool him. You see, last night he was here with me, but now he's drugged and drunk. He drank a lot of alcohol last night and so, as I have his cell phone in one of my hands, in the other I've got the USB drive with the file of the novel. I slipped it into my PC and thumbed through the novel and, yes, I have to say that the story is very intriguing. Now, Paolo is wasting his time waiting for the best offer, the one that will offer him a lot of money, but if you were here by the end of the day, I could give you back the file and even arrange for you to meet a friend of mine who is a literary agent, willing to buy the rights and publish the novel in your name within a few days». As I was saying these words I could imagine the sense of greed, of avarice, that already pervaded every single cell of that creature on the other end of the phone, in a city as far away as Milan. A creature that, shortly thereafter, would fall into my net.

«And what do you ask in return?» she asked.

«Nothing, all I need is to savor my revenge on Paolo, to see it finally completed».

«I don't know if I'll be able to be there today. I must make arrangements...»

«Oh, don't worry! I work in a travel agency. I'll book you a seat on the Milan-Ancona flight, departing at 4pm from Malpensa. At the Raffaello Sanzio airport you will find a rental car with a GPS already set to the address of my house in Recanati, where an excellent dinner and the literary agent with a contract ready to sign will be waiting only for you. Give me your e-mail address and by eleven o'clock I'll send you the plane ticket. All you have to do is print it».

I hung up the phone without giving her time to reply. I wanted that, from that moment on, the fire of curiosity, ambition, revenge, would burn in the heart of that witch, consuming her in the waiting for the moment to come to my house.

Before going to the office, I went to the beauty salon and asked the hairdresser to dye my hair copper red.

«Well, of course blond hair with pink streaks doesn't suit your outfit today, but we can't dye it every day, the hair gets damaged, it wears out».

«Then do it with one of those colored shampoos. I'll wash it tomorrow and that will be the end of it. Today the hair must be the color I asked for!»

As soon as I arrived at the office, I organized Aurora Centofanti's trip. At ten o'clock everything was already booked, flight and rental car, but I would not have sent her the email before the appointed time. At this point I was curious to know what Aurora looked like, perhaps out of jealousy rather than curiosity, or perhaps because, given the lesbian relationships I had enjoyed for some time, a new female guest could have stimulated my erotic fantasies. The chick didn't have a Facebook profile, or if she did, it was protected by privacy from those who sought her out and had no relationship with her. I searched on Google images and came up with a nice roundup of close-ups and half busts of many women named Aurora, although not

Centofanti. One image attracted my curiosity: a blonde woman, wavy hair, blue eyes behind a pair of light-rimmed glasses, was reading a book smoking a thin cigarette, a "slim". The caption stated that Aurora Centofanti would have presented her novel in Milan, at the Feltrinelli Bookshop in Via Ugo Foscolo, on February 17, 2012. The news was therefore a couple of years old. If the woman in the photo was really Aurora, I judged that, despite her very fair skin, accentuated by a very strong shade of lipstick, she was a very attractive woman. I simultaneously felt a jealousy and a thrill of desire towards her. To be in line with my workplace policies, I closed the search result and went outside the office to smoke. Unfortunately, two lousy cigarettes from the very old pack failed to satisfy my nicotine needs. Not being able to leave my workplace to go to the tobacconist, I returned to my workstation and sent the e-mail with a plane ticket and travel instructions to Centofanti. Almost immediately I received an e-mail reply confirming that she would be there at the agreed time. The second pawn to be lured into my home for that evening was Carla, and at the end of the evening two other people would come down to the basement of my apartment. For everything to succeed, I had to play it by ear. In Centofanti's eyes, Carla would be the literary agent with a contract in her purse ready to be signed. But it was important that my fiery friend was totally unaware of this.

As I left the office for my lunch break, I rushed to the tobacconist's to buy a packet of real cigarettes, lit one and smoked it in a few intense puffs. I threw the cigarette butt away and immediately lit another one. I was already in front of the real estate agency; inside Carla was still busy sorting out the paperwork. The window was locked, but when my friend saw me, she hurried to let me in, a triumphant smile on her lips. She leaned in to kiss me, and I let her.

«I figured you'd be back sooner or later. The other night was so sudden, so intense, it was wonderful. You can't escape our relationship. You desire me as much as I desire you», and she threw herself at me in search of a new voluptuous experience, which I could barely avoid.

«Yes, I know, perhaps it is true. But not now, and not here! I need to talk to you; how about we go get a bite to eat together somewhere?»

«I'll go for the organic food restaurant then; you know, I'm a firm health nut». In contrast to what she was saying, she lit a cigarette and was about to leave, probably struggling to put aside her erotic instincts for the moment.

In front of a colorful plate in which one could recognize grains, raw and cooked vegetables, legumes, a few morsels I imagined could be fish, and seaweed and fresh and dried fruits, it was difficult for me to be inspired to take a single bite. Instead, the food delighted my friend's palate. I wondered how I would have been treated if I had asked for a plate of spaghetti amatriciana style. Probably they would have politely invited me to leave. The environment was muffled, the waiters polite and obsequious and a piped music system allowed you to listen to relaxing music, bordering on lullabies. I took a bean and brought it to my mouth, trying to repress the gag of vomit that, like a reflex arch, was trying to make sure that the "stuff" did not reach my poor stomach. Putting on a good face, I threw my bait towards Carla.

«The other night you were a tornado, a cyclone. I wasn't able to keep you down. Instead, I think this is the right environment to talk to each other calmly and serenely. You see, I haven't abandoned the idea of selling my apartment here in Recanati and moving to Ancona. And I would really like for you, through your agency, to make the sale. I have already signed the offer for additional guaranties for the purchase of the new apartment, and therefore I will soon need a certain economic liquidity, which can only come from the sale of my current home. Your real estate agency is the most accredited here in town. I know you will not disappoint me in this».

Carla, listening, continued to chew slowly and hold the ingredients of the macrobiotic menu in her mouth for a long time. I imagined it had to be done that way to avoid regurgitating it all immediately, but I didn't have the courage to bring anything else to my mouth. My friend, however, seemed satisfied with the food, and I took advantage of her apparent tranquility to continue my speech.

«Yes, you're right, I too need to continue to see you, to experience the urges and drives that unite us, to indulge in the voluptuousness and understanding that can exist only between two women. But I also need to get away from this country, to have a more varied, more open life. But this will not preclude the possibility of continuing to see each other. I'm not going to live in a distant city. Ancona is only twenty kilometers away. My house will be open for you, as I believe yours will be for me. And then I will certainly continue to work at Angelo's travel agency, at least until I find something better. I will then be here in Recanati every day, and we can meet as often as we like».

Carla nodded, sighed, swallowed what she had in her mouth, then replied a little wistfully.

«As much as Ancona is not a city like Milan or Rome, it's still a big city. You will find opportunities, with men or with other women. And then I know that you will get further and further away from me, until you completely disappear. But that's okay, let's live our passion while it lasts, and keep our feet in the present. What do you want me to do for you?»

«Come tonight at dinner time to my house. There will also be another guest, someone from Milan, perhaps interested in buying the apartment. If you bring the letterhead of the real estate company, it is possible that we could get a sale agreement tonight. In any case, I would like you to prepare an exclusive contract, in which I will give full mandate to your agency to sell my property, even making it available immediately. Do you think you can prepare it tonight? If the sale does not go through with my guest, I will sign the contract and give you the keys to the house right away. Tomorrow I'll pack up my things and move to Ancona; maybe for a few days I'll stay in a hotel, at the Hotel Dorico, before settling into my new home».

«You are very determined, Emanuela! All right, I'll prepare everything you asked for and be at your place tonight at eight o'clock sharp».

To seal the deal, I provoked her. Under the table, I slipped my foot out of my shoe and reached for her leg. Knowing that the tablecloth was long enough to cover our mischief, I caressed her leg with my foot, up and up, until I reached the mount of Venus. I could see her doing everything she could to try not to start moaning, moaning with pleasure and desire. At one point she stood up abruptly.

«I have to go to the bathroom for a minute», she said, winking at me.

She was sure I would have joined her, but instead I abandoned her again in the grip of desire. I went to the cash register, paid the bill for both of us, and left.

For now, you'd better masturbate, my dear, then tonight there will be a few surprises, even with my guest in Milan. I composed this sentence as a text message on my cell phone and sent her the SMS. The text message arrived almost immediately, with an animated figure attached: a hand clenched into a fist from which the middle finger was rhythmically raised.

I deleted that obscene MMS, lit up a cigarette and headed back to my office satisfied. Before I could even get there, the sound of an incoming message came from my cell phone. Another obscenity from the nymphomaniac? No, this time the sender was someone else, Tonino Della Valle.

I read your E-mail and I was intrigued. I will be in Recanati tomorrow evening. Greetings.

I did not hesitate to reply, typing quickly on the touch keyboard.

Great, I'll let you know when and where to meet. A kiss.

Perfect, the circle was getting tighter and tighter, all the pieces were coming together, and at the right time each one would be in its place. I never thought it could happen, and yet it was happening. By Sunday night, Emanuela La Capricciosa would have satisfied her every single whim.

Between one client and another, I spent most of the afternoon writing a long e-mail to Tonino, informing him not only of the homosexual trysts in which his ex-wife had become embroiled in recent times, but also of the drug and sniff parties in which she used to participate. I was careful not to tell him who had been one of her constant companions for some time. I had to come clean. The great thing was that he too, who would have fallen into my trap by now, would have been smeared for life. Instead of a career in the Police, he would have been permanently disbarred from the force! What idiots men are, or at least some men.

They seem so intelligent, but then they fall like ripe pears in front of a woman like me, who knows how to properly use her seduction weapons. A policeman, a detective, who let himself be fooled like that, without even realizing the bluff he was the victim of!

At 6.30 p.m. I didn't even wait for Angelo to come out of the "back store", I shut down the computer, brushed the indecent orange lipstick over my lips, put a cigarette in my mouth and left the office. Walking along Corso Persiani with an unlit cigarette in my mouth, at least three men approached me with lighters in their hands, ready to light it. When the fourth man approached, I gently took the hand coming in contact with me between my two, which gave off an unusual warmth. Slowly, I waited for the stranger to light the flame; I brought it close to the tip of the cigarette, I made sure that it took some time to light, then I brought my face close to the man's and puffed the smoke in his face. Simultaneously I put my hand on his lower abdomen and grabbed his member: «Oh, what a disappointment! So soft? Where have real men gone?»

If just before, that penis was already in the throes of a sudden erection, at those words, I felt it sag under my hand. The guy disappeared, his face burning with shame.

When the doorbell rang, I was still working out the final details for the evening's meeting. I had had little time, but I had changed into a mini black evening dress, which left my bare legs uncovered, no stockings or pantyhose of any kind, patent leather shoes with stiletto heels that made my silhouette even more slender, vermilion lipstick, foundation, and light makeup, which made the features of my face very attractive. I hadn't prepared a real dinner, but appetizers that could be eaten in the living room, without having to set a table. The trays all featured somewhat aphrodisiac food: shrimp cocktail, caviar canapés, oysters, cold pasta salad with white and black truffle shavings, and so on. Champagne was chilled in the bucket full of ice and, to finish, plenty of smoke and coke for everyone. For the Marijuana I had prepared some "bongs" with exotic features, but there was also a hookah, if my guests would have liked a community smoke, rather than one.

When I opened the door, I had to admit that Centofanti was more beautiful and sexier than I had noticed in the photos. The light of the sunset gave her blonde hair a special glow. The woman was almost as tall as me, maybe even taller than me, considering the heels elevating me by several inches. A simple woman in her elegance, the clothing was sober and consisted of jeans and t-shirt, obviously "signed" by well-known designers. Seeing me open, she lowered her large-framed sunglasses and showed me two beautiful blue eyes. I kissed her on the cheeks – I felt like a traitor at that moment - inviting her to come in.

«Be my guest. The other guest will be here any minute», I said, holding out the pack of cigarettes to offer her one. She declined with a wave of her hand.

«Thank you, but I quit smoking a few months ago and would like to keep up that healthy habit. Rather, I would like to go to the bathroom to freshen up».

I pointed the way, regretting that she had refused to smoke. I knew, however, that the VIPs from Milan would have plenty of Coke to go around. Centofanti could not be immune from that "vice". When the time was right, she would have appreciated the snort. While she was in the bathroom, I prepared an aperitif for Aurora, a particular cocktail that would have paved the way for the next steps. Delirium had provided me with everything I had asked for, including ecstasy tablets that could be dissolved in liquids without altering the taste. The bastard had charged a lot, but the "stuff" was of excellent quality. When the girl returned to the lounge, she greedily drank the drink, asserting that it had a particular taste, but it was very pleasant. The effects would manifest themselves later, following the release of serotonin in her brain. I was sure she would then accept to smoke.

Carla didn't take long to arrive, she too was very sexy, she was wearing a burgundy red linen summer suit, and sheer tights slightly amber; she came in with a lit cigarette half consumed and put it out in the ashtray. I introduced the two to each other.

«Aurora Centofanti, the person from Milan I told you about. Carla Bertoni is our agent, Aurora!» That I referred to Carla simply as "agent" meant that while one meant literary agent, the other in her mind associated the adjective real estate with the noun I had spelled out. The two leaned toward each other and shook hands warmly. I noticed Carla's lecherous gaze towards her new acquaintance, and I sensed that she had reciprocated with equal emphasis. Could it be that Centofanti had lesbian impulses too? This would have made my plans much easier, but maybe it was just my impression. My nymphomaniac friend would get busy, and I would help her achieve her goals.

«Did you bring the draft contracts, as I asked, Carla?» I asked my friend, momentarily interrupting the flow of libidinous thoughts towards the other.

«Of course», she replied, bringing her gaze to mine, perhaps realizing I too was at that moment a tasty morsel to satisfy her sexual hunger. «Just as you asked: a standard contract and the letterhead to eventually draw up an ad hoc one for Mrs. Centofanti here...»

«Oh, go ahead and call me Aurora and call me by my first name. I see we are all of the same age here, more or less, and I don't see any reason to have unnecessary formalities».

This statement had satisfied Carla's subconscious; she took a glass with the aperitif, invited the two of us to do the same and raised her own in a toast: «To our new acquaintance and to the conclusion of this contract, then!»

«Yes», I interjected, trying to keep Carla from getting too out of line and revealing her identity as a real estate agent. «But before we talk business, let's honor the delicacies I've prepared».

After eating and drinking, the euphoria of both my guests, and my own, was through the roof. I invited Aurora and Carla to sit with me in the living room armchairs, while I, on the side of the couch, busied myself with preparing the hookah set up in the center.

«You didn't agree to the cigarettes, Aurora, but you have to agree to smoke this with us», I said handing her one pipe, from which a trickle of vapor mixed with Marijuana smoke was already escaping. «As everywhere else in the world, hospitality is sacred in my house, and I would be offended to death if you did not accept».

«What's in it?» she asked curiously, grabbing the pipe, and bringing it closer to her face.

«Oh, aromatic essences; the smoke is very good and pleasant. And it doesn't hurt like cigarettes», I lied, although I had mixed very strong essences with the herb. She brought the pipe to her mouth and inhaled. On the other side, Carla had taken several greedy puffs and was already enveloped by the exhaled smoke.

«Everything great», Carla affirmed, now almost out of it. «Your hospitality is always top notch, Emanuela. But I bet it doesn't end there. I bet you can offer us some of that top-quality white powder, too, can't you? Where did you hide it today?» She stood up and walked over to the heavy curtain, peeling it back and uncovering the security door. «Golly! In the safe? That must be some over-the-top stuff!»

«No, there are other things there. Maybe even an especially valuable USB flash drive», and I turned my complicit gaze towards Centofanti, who nodded to signify that she understood. «I'll open that door for you soon, but first...»

I took out some envelopes from a drawer and carefully prepared the lines on the living room table, three for each guest and one for me. I handed the twenty-euro bills to Carla and Aurora, noting with interest the writer's ability to roll the paper and suck up the powder. Maybe she had used the cocaine several times get inspired for creative writing, who knows! The two, who by now treated each other like old friends, had launched into a discussion about high fashion from Milan. While they were talking about dresses, skirts, decorated tights and so on, I was waiting for the right moment to open the security door and give the two unsuspecting victims access to the secret part of my house. At a certain point I heard the doorbell ring. Who could it be? I was tempted not to open the door, to pretend that no one was home, but I realized that it was impossible not to hear from the outside the stupid cries coming from those two chickens in the living room every so often. The hallway was dark, I pulled down the curtain of a window, peeked out and recognized the newcomer. Wow, how could he already be there? I had to find a valid excuse to make him leave. I opened the door a crack.

«Tonino? I was not expecting you until tomorrow, how come you're already here?»

«Well, I was so curious I couldn't wait any longer, so I asked for half a day of leave and, even if there were no direct planes from Turin to Ancona, I managed to get one from Milan, and I arrived about two hours ago. I read your emails on the plane with my tablet, and I got even more curious. So, as soon as I landed, I took a cab and here I am. The taxi driver knew you, he is probably a client of your travel agency, and he brought me right here to your house. Isn't that great? I can't wait for you to tell me all about it, in full. Come on, let me in... But you're not alone, I hear other voices, female voices I guess!»

«There are, indeed. Over there is Carla, and it's not appropriate for you to meet now», I said, trying to speak softly. «I invited her tonight just to set the stage for you. I had no idea you were going to get here today. I'll tell you what; go spend a couple of hours somewhere, I don't know, a club, a bar, wherever, then come back here. No one will be here anymore, and you can spend the night at my place. Would you like that idea?»

I looked at him with the most seductive gaze I was capable of, he squared me from head to toe, dwelling on my eyes, my cleavage, my legs. «Yes, I think it could be really interesting. But do you dress like that when you invite other women? Given then the tendencies you told me about my ex-wife...»

«That's the trap. I'm pretending to seduce her so that you can then catch her in the act tomorrow night. It will work, you'll see. Come back in exactly two hours and I'll explain everything».

«Fine, but make sure you don't change your clothes!»

I locked him out of the door, hoping he wouldn't keep hanging around there. I was sure he would do what I suggested. I returned to my guests and judged them to be "cooked to perfection".

«It's hot in here», I said lighting a cigarette, and lowering the straps of my dress which, no longer supported, slid to the floor. I was now in my bra and panties. I invited the others to do the same. They didn't ask twice. I offered each one of them a special cigarette, which I had made Paolo smoke the night before. I lit the cigarettes for them. This time there was no hint of refusal from Aurora, who at that moment was inhaling and exhaling smoke with gusto.

«Good», I resumed, inviting Carla and Aurora to follow me. «It's time to open the security door».

I typed in the combination, opened the door, invited the two to go down the stairs, resealed the room and went down too, reaching the white room. Aurora Centofanti was already looking at the computer on the table with some interest, while Carla was looking at the half-naked body of her potential prey, but also at mine. Her gaze never stopped bouncing from one to

the other, and then lingering on the details of her sur-
roundings.

«Is that where you downloaded the file?» said Aurora curiously, pointing to the white Mac with the now
darkened screen. She was about to tap the mouse,
when I stopped her, gently taking her hand.

«Everything in its own time. Let us first complete
the evening by devoting ourselves to our pleasure. A
pleasure that between women, sometimes, you can
live more intensely than with companions of the op-
posite sex. Right, Carla?»

Carla nodded, while I gently touched Aurora's
pale skin and tried to find the fastening of her bra with
my hand, unhooking it and taking off the garment. I
then took her hand and guided her to unfasten and remove mine. Carla didn't think twice about going bare-
breasted, quickly removing hers, spinning it around
and throwing it in the air with a blatant gesture. I took
a remote control from the drawer of the table and, by
pressing a button, I caused the door to open into the
green and blue room. I took my two guests by the
hand, one on each side, and led them inside.

«Make yourselves comfortable», I told them,
pointing to the large double bed with its fresh, inviting
sheets in the same colors as the room. Still with the
remote control, I turned on a big screen where fractals
appeared in the same shades of colors, projecting a
soft light in the room, making it almost surreal, accompanied by sensual music at a moderate volume.
From the bar fridge I took the bottle of whiskey, I

poured some in two glasses, I slipped in each one another ecstasy pill, and I handed them to each. While the two took off each other's panties, I gained my position in the white room, locking my two new prisoners in their alcove, not before picking up the last of their clothes from the floor and taking them with me. I re-started the white computer from its stand-by mode and, on the screen, appeared windows receiving images from the webcams placed in the rooms. I zoomed in on the window related to the room that had just received the new guests, who I don't think even realized they were trapped, so busy were they in their effusions. I turned on the audio and could see the yelps of those two bitches far exceeded the volume of the music in the room. I then shifted my attention to the black room. It was dark, but the infrared webcam allowed me to see what was going on in there. Paolo had woken up and was wandering around the room naked like a caged lion. Probably accustomed to the darkness, he had spotted a door with a panic bar, and was trying repeatedly, but without success, to open it. Through the PC I gave him the command to open another door, the one that would take him back to the red room. When he heard the click and saw the chink of light, he rushed towards the unlikely escape route. He glanced at the oysters, champagne, and langoustine cocktail on a tray on the bedside table. I saw him give in to his hunger and put the crack of an oyster in his mouth. Then he rummaged around the room.

«No use looking, you'll never find your clothes anyway!» I said to myself contentedly, enjoying the scene. «And now, the master touch». I turned on the big screen in his room, where the images of Carla and Aurora making love to each other appeared. Paolo, at the moment, was astonished to recognize his two ex-girlfriends having a good time together, but almost immediately I noticed his member becoming turgid and reaching an erection. No man can resist seeing two women having sex with each other. I looked at my watch, scheduled the opening of the door that would connect the red room with the green and blue room for about half an hour later, and went back into the living room, closing the security door behind me again. The Mac would store in video tracks everything that happened in those rooms. When I heard the door-bell ring, I realized I was in my underwear. I slipped on a short, see-through robe and went to answer the door.

«You didn't keep your promise!» exclaimed Tonino, observing my breasts thanks to the transparencies of my meager clothing. «You changed your clothes».

«But this way I think you like me even more!» I replied, pulling him in and enveloping him like an octopus.

CHAPTER 6

Saturday, blue, lust

I woke up on the couch with a notable headache. A few hours of sleep, combined with the emotions I had experienced and the substances I had taken, had played a nasty trick on my physical safety. I took a few moments to realize I was still naked and to remember what had happened in the previous hours. I stood up, feeling an unusual sense of freedom walking around the house naked. Before putting on any clothes, I went to the kitchen to make myself an ultra-strong coffee. Then I went to the closet to carefully select the clothing for the day, a crucial day at the end of which my revenge would almost be complete. For the moment I already had four guests in my "secret apartment", two men and two women, who could interact as they pleased in an environment isolated from the rest of the world but guarded by a myriad of cameras and strictly controlled by a powerful computer system. A forced "Big Brother", whose protagonists could discuss, argue, or have sex depending on the dynamics established, also considering the close relationships that had bound them, in times more or less distant, between them. With a variant, compared to the classic Big Brother: the participants had been forcibly stripped bare, and it was therefore difficult to hide any impulses from the housemates. An embarrassing situation, difficult to manage. But, once the inherent shame that everyone feels showing themselves naked in front of others was put aside, it was easy for all participants to be more sincere both in their actions and conversations. A naked person, just for the fact of being in that condition, will never lie, will never tell lies.

I couldn't resist peeking at what was going on, down there, at that moment. Thanks to the connection of the computer system with my I-phone, even from the display of the latter I could see the images sent by the webcams. That was a moment of inactivity; almost everyone was asleep, except Tonino, who was wandering between the orange room and the green and blue one, probably trying to understand how he got into that situation, but especially how stupidly he had fallen into a trap. Carla and Aurora were sleeping wrapped around each other like two kitties in the big bed. At their feet, sideways, lay Paolo, who had taken advantage of the bodies of both after the door between his room and theirs had been opened on command. Tonino, after making love upstairs, aware of what he was doing, had been drinking and smoking, taking drugs and hallucinogenic substances without his knowledge. He hadn't even realized that, by now all naked himself, I had led him to the basement. I had made him approach the computer and showed him the images coming from inside the other rooms.

«Can you see how your ex-wife is having a good time? With men and with other women, as she always did during and after your marriage. You will have this video tomorrow, and you can use it for the purposes of your divorce, but on one condition. Then you will marry me, and you will love and respect me for the rest of your life, until death do us part...», and I resumed making love to him there, giving him my body in front of that PC, on whose screen scrolled the images of Carla, Aurora and Paolo mating with each other in the most incredible and impossible ways. When I felt he was about to reach orgasm, I moved away from him, I commanded the opening of the door of the orange room, I let him in believing we would have finished the intercourse there, but instead I locked him in. From the loudspeakers, I told him: «It's time for you to participate in the ex-boyfriends' party...», and I commanded the opening of the door communicating with the blue and green room. Then I stayed in front of the video to enjoy the sexual evolutions of those four worms, now subjected, for the moment, to my will. Soon they would all become self-conscious again and they would quarrel among themselves, throwing in each other's face events that had happened long ago. And this phase, perhaps, would prove even more interesting than the previous one. But now I had to get dressed.

I carefully chose a one-piece, sleeveless, foot-length dress with a wide slit in the front, midnight blue in color. I paired it with a light blue pantyhose, and even found a strange hat of the same color, under which I hid my hair. I loaded my lips with lipstick, which partly transferred to the filter of the cigarette I went to put in my mouth. I looked for Carla's bag; I finally found it in the confusion that reigned supreme in the living room and, instead of slipping out of it the documents interesting me, I decided that bag matched the outfit I had just worn, and left the room with it. I made sure that into the bag there was the set of keys that would give me access to Carla's agency, as well as cigarettes and a lighter, slipped my set of keys into it and went out. Before heading towards the center of town, I called the cleaning and moving company I had contacted earlier, giving them the go-ahead to take away all the furniture, temporarily cramming it into their storage, until my new home in Ancona was available, and then clean the apartment. Upon my return I would find the house bare, and this was also part of my plan. I could have easily forged the contracts in my office, where I had a very good scanner and a powerful computer at my disposal. But the fact I could do it right in Carla's agency, and with her tools, would have been a considerable advantage I hadn't even considered.

Although I was running late, I stopped at the usual café for breakfast. I sat at a small table, making sure the front slit of my dress left my legs on display, crossing and re-crossing them continuously. The young waiter was looking at me. I called out to him: «In a respectable bar, it would be nice to place at least one red rose in the center of the table occupied by a classy lady. The service in this place leaves something to be desired!»

I saw him leave with a small smile on his lips and proudly return with a rose in a tall and narrow glass container, which he placed in the center of the table. I let him find me with a cigarette between my lips and he didn't hesitate to light it for me. As soon as it was lit, I dropped it from my lips on purpose; the smoking stick slipped down my dress, crossed my legs, fortunately causing no burns to either the fabric or the pantyhose, and ended up on the floor near the tip of one shoe.

«How clumsy of you!» I said, grabbing him by the black tie that hung from the collar of his short-sleeved white shirt, and pulling him toward me. «I want you to pick up that cigarette and smoke it yourself».

I pulled him further down, his face almost touching my groin area. He protested: «But it fell to the ground, and...»

«The customer is always right», I continued, shaking my head, but also placing a hefty tip for him on the coffee table, a nice fifty Euro bill from Carla's wallet. «Smoke it! All of it, down to the filter!»

He obeyed, smoked it all, overcoming the disgust of it having fallen to the ground and making up for it with the taste that my lipstick had left. He put out the cigarette butt in the ashtray and extended his hand to earn his well-deserved fifty bucks. But I had not been paid in full. I stopped him, grabbing his hand, then I took the brioche filled with cream from the saucer in front of me and I bit into it, so its filling overflowed to dirty my lips, my cheeks, and my chin.

«This cream is sour, taste it please», and I pulled him towards me, making him understand he had to taste the cream covering my face. He looked around awkwardly, hoping that no one who knew him was walking by at that moment. And instead, someone, from a remote corner of the square, with a garbled voice, said the phrase he never wanted to hear: «Andrea, you're also involved with forty-year-old women? Take it easy, buddy? Go take a cold shower! Ah ah ah!»

The young man was now red and sweaty from head to toe. Still pulling him by the tie, I pulled his face close to mine and, as fast as a lightning bolt, I stuck my tongue in his mouth.

«Did you taste that? It's sour!» I told him, standing up, taking the bill back, slipping it into my cleavage and finally letting him go. «You don't deserve anything, boy!»

I took long strides toward the real estate agency, my longish thighs sticking out of the front slit of my blue dress with each step. Looking down, I observed my legs the same color of the tights I wore. Blue like the night, blue like desire, a desire to indulge in another of the deadly vices: lust. I was ready to face my guests that night fulfill my plan, before seeing them fall into the trap of my revenge.

I slipped the key into the lock of the window, opened it carelessly, not caring about who was watching me. It did not matter if they were watching me or a person that did not quite belong there! The very fact of acting naturally and carelessly would have aroused no suspicion; those who set their eyes on me were doing so only to admire a splendid specimen of a human female, and I could only feel flattered by that. I felt several male eyes come to touch and even caress my body, but I did nothing, as it was time to face other commitments. I started the PC and made sure that the scanner connected could be suitable for my purposes. But at a certain point, the computer emitted a long beep. I had to enter the password to log in. I didn't even think about it and typed in my name, EMANUELA. Almost by a miracle, the desktop appeared.

Using the PC and the agency's letterhead, following the fake line of the document Carla had prepared the night before, I prepared an exclusive contract in which I, Emanuela Brandimarti, gave an exclusive mandate with full accessibility to the property, for its sale, to the Caporalini Carla e C. s.r.l. Real Estate Agency. The date was several days prior, consistent with the fact that the owner of the agency could well have authorized the work to obtain the underground spaces. I had contacted a trusted company, based far away from Recanati; the work had been carried out in great secrecy and I had also paid a surplus for the discretion of the company itself, which had not even issued an invoice made out to my real name. At the end of the work, I scanned the document that bore Carla's signature at the bottom, made a copy/paste of it on the new document to be printed, threw the latter to a high-definition laser printer, and waited for the result. Great, the signature looked original, but to dispel any doubts, I looked on the desk for an agency stamp and affixed it there, then I signed the document in my own hand in the space provided. I made photocopies and slipped them into what I thought would be an appropriate spot in the agency's archives, while I went to insert the original in an envelope on which I wrote my name in block letters with a black marker: EMANUELA BRANDIMARTI.

It had taken me some time to complete that work, but I was satisfied. It was almost lunchtime, but I had no appetite, or perhaps I had appetite for something other than food. But to appease that appetite several more hours would have to pass. At that point I had to reach Ancona and prepare the ground for the Hotel Dorico. Once the evening had passed as planned, I could no longer return to my home in Recanati. Therefore, my visit to the hotel had two purposes: to book a room that would accommodate me for a few days, while I waited to move to my new residence in Ancona, and to reserve a small room for the following evening's meeting with the last pawn in the game, photographer Leonardo Gerbilli. I wasn't very inclined to use a car, I preferred to walk or take public transportation, but I couldn't help but use it. For some time now I had stored my Mercedes class A in a garage for a fee, also because the garage of my house had been used as part of the secret underground rooms. I got my vehicle and, without even thinking to get something to eat, I reached the Doric city[1]. During the journey, the interior of the Mercedes would have practically turned into a gas chamber, if not for the air conditioning. Noticing that for about three hours, the time I had been inside the real estate agency, I had not smoked, I lit up one cigarette after another in the car until I finished the packet in Carla's purse and started another that I bought before leaving.

I quickly took care of my business in Ancona, but by the time I got back to Recanati and brought the car back to the garage, it was already late afternoon. It was time to call Delirium. The guy didn't even give

---

[1] Ancona is also called Doric city, as it was founded by people of Greek origin, called Dorics (Translator's note).

me time to speak: «Did you like the goods? I still have plenty if you need it. Your party is tonight, right?»

«Some of my guests have already arrived, and some have particular tastes. They would like very young veal meat, and I know you can procure that».

«How do you know about it?» he asked, after a few moments of embarrassed silence. «It's a risky item to handle, it can really hurt, and not just your stomach, so I reserve it for a few trusted customers. Are you sure you want to order it? I can give it to you, but at a high price».

«My dear friend, you know very well these days I spare no expense», I continued to taunt him in a persuasive voice.

«All right, I happen to have a young heifer, just under the age, with tender, juicy meat. But I'll make the delivery myself. Tell me what time, I know your address.»

«Perfect, I was just going to ask you for home delivery. I guess 10 pm would be fine. If you want, you can stay for "dinner" too, how about that? I'll treat you to filly meat if you like it. Meat that is a bit tough, but that will certainly delight your fine palate».

«As long as it's raw, and with lots of lemon on top», he snickered. «I'll be on time and bring the goods you requested. See you later!»

Well, I had done it. And by that evening, my guests would increase to six, including an underage prostitute. Since Delirium had said "just underage", I was hoping for a girl of about seventeen, almost eighteen. But I wasn't sure of the scoundrel's word. Even he eventually fell victim to my vengeance; at least he would stop dealing in that business, which made me sick. I have always considered the exploitation of prostitution, especially child prostitution, as one of the most serious crimes, much more serious than drug dealing, which in some ways I could tolerate a little more, since I had also used them. Had the government passed the soft drug trade, we would not have needed certain individuals in our society. We would have gone to the tobacconist's to buy a packet of Marijuana and that's that. Instead, despite all the political debates, we still must resort to an outlaw and pay a lot more to satisfy a pleasure of ours, which causes no more harm than a pack of cigarettes. Crazy!

When I entered my apartment and saw it almost bare, I felt a knot in my throat I had to repress; the lump traveled to my stomach then came back to my throat. It was a state of sadness, of nostalgia, for something that I had put together with effort and that, in a short time, had vanished. I looked around: the only thing left in the living room was an old and shabby wicker rocking chair, the kitchen had not been touched, as it was custom made for that room, and I had asked to the moving company not to touch it, for it was to be sold with the property. I checked that in the bedroom, inside the built-in closet, was my clothing. Not much, but it wasn't the time to give in to sentimentality, it was time for me to indulge in the vice of lust, taking advantage of the company I had so far put together. I checked my watch, eight o'clock exactly, pulled back the curtain, opened the security door and went downstairs. I got rid of my clothes and, taking advantage of the small wardrobe I had prepared in the computer room, I put on a tiny white shirt, decorated all over with the dollar sign, the U.S. currency, long enough to barely cover my lower abdomen. I observed with narcissistic admiration my long thighs with smooth skin, perfectly shaven a few days ago, and I made sure that the back of the tiny panties slipped into the gap of my ass. At that moment, that was annoying, but it would certainly have proven worthful later on. I lit a cigarette and stood in front of the PC screen. At that moment the red room, the green and blue room, and the orange room were communicating with each other, but all the guests, beautiful naked as nature had created them, were gathered in the room equipped with a double bed. Paolo was lying on the bed and had partly covered himself with the sheet. He was smoking and was observing the two women who, sitting nearly at the same bed, were having a lively discussion between them. They had had plenty of time to get to know each other and discover their true identities. They had gone through a phase of accusing each other, maybe even telling each other many things, until they decided that the person who had led them into a trap was me. And now they were holding each other, consoling each other.

«She's going to kill us, she lured us here to kill us, all four of us», said Centofanti with tears streaking her face.

«Yeah», Carla replied, wiping the tears away from her new friend with her hand, first caressing her face, and then gently descending to more intimate parts. «We all fell for it like fools. We might as well take advantage, while we're still alive, to enjoy intensely the time we have left».

«No, we can't give up like this, there has to be a way out of here!» said Tonino, wandering around the room relentlessly, his cock darting between his legs.

I moved the mouse pointer to a button on the control panel of the sophisticated software, marked N2O. Nitrous Oxide invaded the room from the air conditioning vents, and its effect soon showed on my guests. Also known as laughing gas, Nitrous Oxide has anesthetic and hallucinogenic powers and is considered a mild drug. Inhaled gradually, it causes euphoria and confusion due to the alteration it causes in the nervous communication at the synapse's level. It was time to see if what I had read about this gas would actually happen in reality. And it seemed it did. Paolo, still lying on the bed, had responded to what Tonino had said just before.

«In the black room... Ahahahah... there is a panic bar, it should be... Ihihihih... an emergency exit that leads to the outside, but... ahahahahahahah....» Paolo started to cry, to writhe with laughter, not holding back anymore he got up from the bed, discovering his penis incredibly with a strong erection. He approached Tonino, who was also under the effect of the gas.

«What the hell do you have in place of a cock?... Uhuhuhuh... A love sword?... Ahahahah...», she told him, taking it in her hands and causing it to become even more swollen. Paolo, feeling grabbed, gave pelvic thrusts, as if to encourage masturbation by the other man. The two women were laughing their asses off, touching each other, kissing, lapping their skin and private parts with their tongues.

«So... Ahahahah...», resumed Tonino, referring in a disconnected way to what they were talking about earlier. «Why didn't you run away from the emergency exit if you had the chance?... Ihihih... Maybe because you'd rather stay to fuck my ex-wife? Or your ex-girlfriend? Or both? Ahahahahah...."

«I didn't even know they were here... Ihihihih... I only came to win back my ex-wife, and instead look at the situation I'm in... Uhuhuh... But how can you laugh in this situation? We must try to go back to the black room, Tonino... Ahahaha... You are a policeman... Ihihihih...».

The two men, to get closer to the door that led to the black room, approached the two women, who were carelessly emitting incredible screams and laughter. The door had no handle and, despite Tonino's and Paolo's attempts, it would not give way. The two men, with their members erect to the maximum, almost to the limit of explosion, turned their attention to the women.

«Ahahah...», resumed Tonino. «Why instead of continuing to be fags and lesbians, don't we devote ourselves to sex as Christ commands? You take my wife Paolo, who I prefer the Milanese VIP... Uahahahahah... Uahahahahuuuh...»

The moment has come to enter the scene, not without having first given the commands to the PC to interrupt the flow of Nitrogen Oxide at nine forty-five, and replace it with that of anesthetic gas, Isoflurane, which soon would put my guests in sleep.

I unlocked the door to the blue and green room and entered, abandoning myself too to the voluptuousness of the laughing gas. I tried to regulate my breathing to inhale as little of it as possible, but it wasn't easy, as the room was now saturated with it. Both men and women, though still laughing, looked at me strangely. I spun around so everyone could admire my firm buttocks, cleverly highlighted by the tiny clothing I had just worn and threw myself into the fray.

«Has our time come? Ahahahah... Have you come to kill us?» Tonino asked, while Carla and Aurora, frightened were once again hugging each other, terrified although they continued to laugh under the effect of the gas.

«Yes, I could kill you, but I won't, at least for now... First... I want to get my satisfaction from you. Death would be too easy a solution, wouldn't it?» I looked at them one by one trying to barely hold back my laughter. «You, Tonino, in your life you have never possessed my body, not even last night even if you were close to it, so the time has come to do it, now, here, in front of the others, in front of your ex-wife, my ex-husband and the Milanese VIP you like so much.»

I took off my panties, thus getting rid of the annoyance they were causing me, and I approached Tonino. The others clearly did not hold back and the sexual fantasy of all five of us made sure that in the next sixty minutes, on that double bed, free rein was given to all those perversions that each of us holds within ourselves but never has the courage to put into action with our partner, official or occasional as it may be. At a certain point I felt myself being penetrated simultaneously in front by Paolo and behind by Tonino, while Carla was pushing her tongue into my mouth and Aurora was caressing and kissing my breasts. I don't know how that intertwining of bodies had been achieved, also because, under the effect of gas, I no longer had a great conception of space and time. We were all thinking about laughing and enjoying. Only the brief sound of a small alarm made me realize it was time to get out. I hurriedly put back on my blouse and panties and left the others still in the grip of their desires, still not satisfied. But after a while they would have collapsed like four little angels.

I had just enough time to recover from my daze, put on a short denim skirt and a sober short-sleeved blouse, and go back upstairs, when the doorbell rang. It was Delirium, accompanied by a young black girl, thin, slender, a fabulous body, full lips, dark eyes, but who looked no more than fifteen, sixteen years old.

I looked her over from head to toe and then turned to Delirium: «Are you sure she is just under the age? And that she is here in Italy legally? I wouldn't want to get in trouble because of you».

«What do you care about the details? You don't have to account to anyone, just cater to the tastes of your guests. The girl is Senegalese, her family needs a lot of money, and you can get them some, thanks to me. Besides, she is beautiful and experienced. Get undressed, Alma, show your body to our client...». The girl let the little dress she was wearing slip to the floor, showing off her body, the smooth and very shiny ebony skin, two firm and well-made breasts, with the huge areolas typical of black women. She turned to Delirium, asking him for a cigarette, he gave it to her and lit it, then the man looked around, observing the half-empty apartment: «But what happened here, did a tornado pass by? I don't see your guests, nor do I see where you could accommodate them. What are you doing, ripping me off?»

«No, it's just that I'm moving, I'm moving to Ancona. My guests are in the "guest house", I said, pulling back the curtain and showing him the stairs that led downstairs. «But first, since you kept your word and brought the heifer, I want to keep my word to you and let you taste the filly meat, of *this* filly».

I invited Alma to go downstairs and wait there for us touching nothing. She obeyed and disappeared down the stairs, naked as she was, without even hinting at putting her dress back on. I took Delirium by the hand and led him into the kitchen.

«I hope you've brought more bags of that good quality powder. I think my guests are starting to run out and we don't want them to miss it», I said, pulling lemons out of the fridge and looking for the juicer, finally finding it after opening two or three kitchen doors.

As I squeezed the lemons, he pulled two sachets out of his pockets, made lines on the cupboard shelf, and invited me to snort along with him.

«Excellent, as always», I stated, slipping off my blouse and handing him the lemon juice. «You said you'd like your meat raw and with lots of lemon on it. Come on, then!»

He didn't make me say it twice, poured the juice over my breasts and began the tasting. In fact, I was disgusted to be touched by that dirty individual. I let him do it for a while, then, when I felt that with his hand was trying to lift my skirt, I interrupted him: «I think that, as a taste, may be enough. Come, let's not keep the others waiting».

Even if he wasn't convinced, he composed himself, I put my blouse back on and we went downstairs, where Alma, like a faithful dog, was waiting for us patiently. I felt too sorry for that girl; even if she was one pawn of my plan, I should have protected her. She was only there at the appropriate time playing into my hands. I looked at the computer screen again and showed them the guests, who were all sleeping at the moment. Like domesticated cats, numb from the anesthetic gas, they had all gone to their own beds, so the two women were lying on the double bed, Paolo was sleeping in the red room and Tonino in the orange one. I opened the door of the purple room, which communicated internally with the orange room, and let the young prostitute in. On the PC screen, I pointed Tonino out to her: «He is the guest with special tastes. When he wakes up, he can open the door that connects your rooms to each other. Satisfy him properly and you'll get a more than generous reward».

The girl slipped inside the room, and I closed the door behind her, seeing her image appear on one of the monitor windows. Delirium turned rather arrogantly, «I'll take care of her. Don't promise her anything directly. Rather, we agreed that the fee would be up front, it's time for you to cough up the money!»

«What a rush! You may receive fees that are even different, beyond the simple money I will not fail to liquidate. You see, now my guests are exhausted, but...» I recalled on the screen sequences of the films showing the sexual evolutions of Carla and Aurora and some moments when we had all coupled together, including myself. «We're going to resume dancing in a little while. Don't you want to dance too? You could take advantage of those two, they're horny. And then me too, you've had a taste, why not finish the meal?»

With these words, I commanded the opening of the door of the yellow room. I pushed him in and closed the door behind him, sealing it. I activated the big screen inside his room, and simply said to him, «Good luck, you bastard!»

«Bitch, you tricked me. Let me out of here now!», and he punched and kicked the door. But from the outside you could hear nothing; the soundproofing had been done to perfection.

CHAPTER 7

Sunday, yellow, sloth

Rather than waking up, I regained consciousness in the rocking chair. I don't know how I got there. In my right hand, abandoned on the outside of the chair's armrest, was a lit cigarette half consumed, while an ashtray containing already several cigarette butts lyed on the floor, under my same hand. I was wearing a pair of jeans and a blouse I had found who knows where. They were not my size; probably in my state of mental confusion, I had slipped into Centofanti's clothes. I crushed my cigarette in the ashtray and groped for the packet on the floor, immediately lighting another. I could reason, but I couldn't find the strength to get up from that rocking chair. Yet there were things to do! I should have cleaned the house of all the objects that belonged to me and that could compromise the success of the operation. I would have had to retrieve the scattered clothes of my guests and store them properly in the closet of the white room. I would then have to carefully cut from the video recordings captured by the computer all the sequences in which I appeared. Then I would have to dress appropriately and reach Ancona, after having picked up my car at the garage and having disposed of all the compromising material. It seemed my brain was working, but the impulses coming from it could not adequately command the actions to be done to my body, which remained inert on that chair, able only to continue to light the last remaining cigarettes. A condition I associated with the last of the deadly vices, sloth, and with the color yellow, the color to which I would have tuned my clothing if only I could move. Images of what had happened the night before ran through my mind. I had commanded the opening of the door between the purple room and the orange room, and Alma had slipped into the bed of sleeping beauty, to complete the task entrusted to her. I trusted that Tonino had respected the moral rules that required him not to have sex with a minor, but under the influence of drugs, these were probably inhibited. So, when he woke up from his torpor and found himself next to the new unexpected young guest, he had immediately caressed her dark skin. And he would have violated her too, after all those who had been there before, if I hadn't injected anesthetic gas into his room again. Not that the girl was a virgin, but I couldn't bear to be the one responsible for what would happen to her in there. But I waited for Carla, Aurora and Tonino to recover from their torpor, then I connected their rooms with the one I had let Delirium into. Delirium, seeing the naked bodies of the two women, forgot he had been lured into a trap, emptied his pants pockets, and put in several "doses" to be shared with his new companions; he also got rid of his shirt, remaining shirtless. I vaporized again in their rooms the Nitrogen Oxide, so fun was assured. After a while, I couldn't resist, and I satiated the desire for lust that had been my main attraction for the day. From the moment I had walked through the door of the blue and green room, I had no more memories. But the important thing was that I had gone out and locked my guests up for good, each one in his own room, each isolated from the others, except for the two women, who, once they had regained consciousness, would have accused each other again and would have argued heavily between themselves. Or maybe they would have agreed and maybe they would have resumed groping each other. That was their business, I didn't care anymore. From the moment I left, I would have commanded the PC to stop recording video. But the webcams would still be active, and I could always control the situation in the "house" with my iPad.

Only after finishing my cigarettes, I found the strength to get up from the rocking chair and get dressed. I had to be ready for the game of strip poker, so the clothing, besides yellow, had to include all the accessories provided by the game for women: stockings, garters, panties, bra, petticoat, shoes, skirt with belt, half-sleeved shirt, light jacket, scarf, handbag, and hat. Each chip in the game would represent a garment. At the end, the loser would have to remove all the clothes and accessories corresponding to the lost chips. I paid particular attention to the makeup, and at the end I realized that I had woken up, I had shaken off the sense of sluggishness, of apathy, that had gripped me until a short time before. After taking care of the computer and the guests' clothes, I quickly gathered my few remaining belongings. I took one last peek at the inhabitants of the "house" from the PC monitor: who was sleeping, who was wandering around the room in the grip of his mental lucubration or wondering if he would ever get out of there alive, or how long he would be locked up. Tonino compulsively opened the small fridge-bar in the fruitless hope of finding something to eat. Carla and Aurora, at that moment were fighting fiercely; I was afraid that they would fight, but at a certain point, the proximity of the two naked female bodies gave way to new caresses, almost an embrace, and then they fought again, more vehemently than before. And so on, in an alternating sequence of hatred and sexual desire, which I don't know what it could have led to. The time had come for me to move away, and permanently, from my home in Recanati. I climbed the stairs, sealed the armored door, and with it its precious contents, placed the two large garbage bags next to the entrance containing the material to be taken away, and quickly walked to pick up my car. I went back, loaded the bags in the trunk and I started towards Ancona. Before reaching my destination, I got rid of the material in a dumpster I thought was at a reasonable distance from Recanati and from the "scene of the crime". I now liked to call my home that, even though no crime had been, nor would have been, committed. But for sure in a few hours, the place would be invaded by policemen and journalists.

The Hotel Dorico was in the center of Ancona, a five-star hotel in a beautiful, elevated position, overlooking the sea and Monte Conero. But beyond its location, the management and the staff were exquisite, but above all, maximum privacy was guaranteed. I went up to the room reserved for me, arranged my few personal belongings, and went to the bathroom mirror to check I looked impeccable.

Leonardo Gerbilli arrived in perfect time and dressed in the manner required by the game we would play. The clothing was heavy for the season, but I had had the hotel management reserve a smoking room for me, where the air conditioning system kept the temperature low and powerful extractor fans, whose hum was unfortunately overwhelming, provided a continuous change of air. As if in perfect synchronicity, not even by chance, we found ourselves in the hall, me coming down from my room, him entering through the main entrance. Leonardo was a man in his mid-forties, rather obese and flabby, his face with a double chin and florid cheeks, his porcine eyes that had settled on the hotel hostess accompanying us to the lounge. A typical man whose job you would have imagined just by looking at him, a man who stirred no physical attraction in me. The management of the hotel, besides the lounge, had put at my disposal two employees, young and good-looking, a girl in her twenties and a man not even thirty, well trained to assisting special customers like us. Once we were introduced to the room, the man opened the lid of the box of Cuban cigars placed on the card table, letting us know that we help ourselves, while the girl unwrapped a new deck of cards and distributed the chips, representing the items of clothing.

«Would you like to play together with us, the four of us, or would you prefer to remain alone?» the girl asked, chopping me a cigar, and lighting it.

I, who knew how the thing worked, but especially that I wanted to play, if possible, before Leonardo tried to dismiss them, replied that we would prefer to play with four people. The photographer refused the cigar that the girl offered him and lit one of his cigarettes. The other man dealt the cards and distributed them. The two hotel employees were well trained to lose, but not constantly. Each hand the girl lost, she would slip off the corresponding garment, and so did the other young man, while our losses were set aside, as we would reserve the right to remove the lost garments only at the end or settle in a purely virtual manner. At one point, the girl was left only in her briefs. Under the lecherous gaze of Leonardo, she took a cigarette from his pack, lit it, and turned to him: «The hotel management does not allow me to play this last chip. If you want the extra, tell the receptionist, ask for room 333, it's a bit expensive, but it's worth it. Leonardo, sweating profusely despite the low temperature, nodded his head following her with his eyes while she disappeared through the back door, a different door from the one we had entered. The man at that point asked to get out of the game as well.

«All right», and I dismissed him, placing a substantial tip in his hand. «No extras for me. I'll settle for finishing the game with my friend. Thanks for everything».

«All right, Leonardo», I said, winking at him. «Now that we're alone, I'd say let's stop playing virtually. Let's take back all our chips and start over. But any clothing lost, must be removed!»

«Alright, deal the cards!»

I re-lighted the cigar that lay resting nearly at the ashtray, dealt the cards and saw that, by changing one card, I could have a full house. I had three fives and a nine. I threw on the table the chips related to the hat, scarf, and belt. Probably Leonardo had good cards too, because he accepted the bet and even raised with his pants. I changed the card and luck gave me a nine.

«I see», I said.

Leonardo, satisfied, discovered a double pair, two sevens and two fours. I showed my full house and saw my opponent take off his first clothes. He lost one hand after the other and, in order, the tie, the shoes, the socks, the shirt and the undershirt flew away. At this point I could admire the individual in all his flaccid roundness. It was certainly not a pretty sight to behold; his whole body was also drenched in sweat. I poured him a shot of double malt whiskey and asked him what he would do, pulling out of my bag a SD memory card, small but able to hold a lot of data.

«If you lose your underwear too, goodbye material. Do you continue or do you want to be like the hotel hostess?»

«There's no one who can forbid me to play the underwear too. Deal the cards!»

From this point on, I started losing, even changing the cards if I had possible winners in my hand. So as Leonardo got dressed, I was losing one garment after another.

«Looks like luck has turned on your side», I stated as I was left already bare-breasted. I was still wearing only my underwear, my stockings, which were no longer supported by the garter belt and slid down my thigh and wrinkle into creases, and my high-heeled shoes. In the next two hands I lost the shoes, thanks to a lucky turn for Leonardo, then the socks, thanks to me discarding a pair of kings.

«Either luck started to turn the right way, or you got distracted from a certain point on, my dear

Emanuela. You have only one garment left. Are you going to play it or are you going to give me the game?» The guy had relaxed and was now sweating much less. Satisfied, he lit a cigarette waiting for my answer

«Not so fast, Leonardo!» I took one last drag from the cigar, puffed a thick cloud of smoke into the air, then stood up, taking my opponent by the hand. Beyond another door was a room with a double bed. I saw him sit nearly at the bed and slip off his pants again. I, facing him, shook my head.

«No, no! That's not what I meant exactly. Well, you win, and you get to decide the reward. Either away with the panties, but see and not touch, as actively having sex was not part of the deal or have the memory card. Decide!»

«Bitch of a female, bastard that you are!» he said, sweating profusely again. «Stop playing with me, put your clothes on and give me the fucking card».

I retrieved my clothes and turned my back to him to put them on. When I turned around again, the guy was still fumbling with the waistband of his pants, which he was struggling to close because of his excessive body weight. I put the memory card in his hand, and he squeezed it contentedly.

«Good!» he exclaimed, beaming with happiness. «I can't wait to see this material and pass it on to the editorial staff of...»

«At the time», I nipped his enthusiasm in the bud. «You don't think it could have been that simple? That card is still blank. If you follow my instructions, in a couple of hours you'll get what you've earned and fill the card with really compromising photos and footage for certain people. And you can't even imagine what characters of undoubted fame you'll find filmed and maybe, if you go to my house, you might be able to photograph them directly yourself in some somewhat daring pose».

«Damn it, Emanuela, you're still playing with me. How can I trust you? So be it, all right. Tell me what else I need to do to get my hands on this material. Let's at least hope it's really worth what you promised».

«Take this cell phone, Leonardo. It's an old model, but suitable for our purposes. There is only one number stored in the address book, to which I will answer you. It is not the user I usually use; you can never have too much caution. Go to my house and enter, you will find the key to the front door inside the meter compartment. When you're inside, call me exclusively with that device and I'll give you the rest of the instructions. Good luck!»

«Drop dead! I hope I can trust you».

I watched him finish quickly arranging his clothes, throw his jacket over one shoulder, avoiding slipping it on as the impact of the outside temperature would reactivate his profuse sweating, and disappear, while I, much more quietly, reached the hotel reception and had my room key handed. I would have spent some time taking a nice shower, also because, after everything that had happened in the last forty-eight hours, I needed one.

I calculated the time and at the right time I opened the App on my I-phone connected to the Mac and to the spy cams scattered outside my home, or rather former home. It was now dark, but the video camera near the front door was sending me good images. Leonardo didn't take long to arrive, he immediately found the key in the counter compartment and entered. Unfortunately, I had not placed a webcam in the living room, so I could not enjoy the amazed face of the guy at the sight of the empty apartment. The phone didn't take long to ring.

«What game are you playing, Manu? Your apartment is completely empty. Either the thieves came by, or you emptied it before you left. So?»

«Don't worry, Leo. I told you I'd give you further instructions. There's a heavy curtain in front of you, pull it aside and you'll see a security door: do you see it?»

«Yes, I see it», he replied, with a sigh.

«Next to the door, on your left, is a keypad. Type in the combination: 0 - 1 - 1 - 4 - 8, then press the green key. The door will unlock».

«Done! There are stairs going down. Do I go down?»

«That's right, Leonardo! Go and you won't regret it».

I saw his image sent back to my phone's display by the webcam of the same PC he was approaching,

«You've found your treasure. You should be good enough to be able to insert the memory card in its port and download all the multimedia material that the machine has recorded in the last few hours».

I saw him fiddle with the PC, quickly scroll through a few sequences, and issue the command to back up the contents onto the memory card. Since the telephone communication was still active, after a few moments of silence, Leonardo turned again.

«I've had a peek and it does indeed look like hot material, especially for a distinguished writer who has recently embarked on a political career. But where are your guests?»

«I know you have prima donna ambitions. Would you like to join them and take shots directly with your camera? On the control panel, hit the "Open indigo room door" command. But close the phone call first, because when you're in there, there will be no cellular communication», I lied through my teeth.

I saw him retrieve the SD card, insert it into his digital camera and give the command to open the door indicated. Well, he was executing what I had imagined to perfection, without even being trained to do so. As soon as he stepped into the indigo-colored room, I took command of the system through my iPad, closed the door behind him and opened all the other doors that allowed the internal rooms to communicate with each other. Leonardo found himself in front of all those characters, more or less known, but above all more or less naked. Only Delirium was wearing pants, Carla had covered herself with a sheet grabbed from one bed, while the others were completely naked. He begun to take pictures like crazy. There was a lot of confusion, my guests felt cheated, they protested for the sudden intrusion, and they claimed their privacy. Someone had tried to throw himself on Leonardo and snatch his camera, but he, thanks to his size, made him fall to the ground. It was time to put an end to that whole charade. I had prepared the "final bang" by hand, following to the letter the instructions I had found on the Internet, but I wasn't sure if it was going to work. I started the call to the cell phone that Leonardo had. The ringing of that device was set on a frequency that would have activated a detonator, which at that moment was close to him. The sequence of explosions was deadly, a smoke bomb exploded in every room, the environment was soon saturated with a thick curtain that prevented me from seeing on the display what was happening. However, I was just in time to see the fire vents that, as expected, sprayed water, soaking the guests, who were panicking.

«We're going to end up like sardines. That bastard is killing us. She wants to burn us in here!» cried Aurora.

«Quick, let's all get to the black room», incited Tonino, who seemed to be the only one who still had some composure. «The fire system probably has an automatic release of the emergency exit!»

«I'm not going out like this, all naked. I want my clothes», Carla complained.

«Better to go out naked than in here roasting, right?» replied Paolo to her.

No one would get hurt. Only smoke had invaded the rooms but, to simulate a dangerous fire even better, I had arranged for the air conditioning system to raise the temperature by several degrees. From my official cell phone, I called 112[2]: «Police? My name is Emanuela Brandimarti. I have a small problem. I haven't been living in my house in Recanati for a few days now, as I have put it on sale and entrusted it to a real estate agency. But now the alarm, which is still active and connected to my cell phone, signals an attempt at intrusion and even a fire. I'm a long way from Recanati, I'm currently staying in a hotel in Ancona, so I can't check on it directly. I'm sure it won't be anything serious, maybe a false alarm, but I would be grateful if you would check it out».

«Of course, of course, it's our duty. I'll send a patrol immediately and I'll also alert the nearest fire station. Keep your phone active, I've registered your mobile number. We will let you know».

I had calculated that a Police patrol, sirens blaring, would take no more than three minutes from the barracks in the center of Recanati to my house in the "Le Grazie" neighborhood. I timed the time, and at the right moment I commanded the release of the pan-

---

[2] Emergency number, like 911 in U.S.A. (Translator's note)

ic bar in the black room. I then activated the reception of images from the webcam placed on the back side of my house. The seven individuals, some naked, some well covered, came out of the back door coughing and crying and were immediately illuminated by the headlight of the Police's gazelle, who, as they realized the situation, called for reinforcements. In a short time, the area was invaded by Police and Police cars, ambulances, even a Civil Defense car, whose staff was distributing blankets, clothes and drinks to the unfortunate victims. The handcuffs were soon snapped on the wrists of Delirium and Leonardo Gerbilli. The others were all in detention, each trying to explain his reasons concisely to a guy dressed in plain clothes, who must have overseen the investigation. When a uniformed policeman reported something to the latter, and Carla Caporalini was handcuffed, I rubbed my hands with satisfaction and closed the connection. Everything had gone as planned, I was satisfied. In seven days, my revenge was complete.

EPILOGUE

Revenge can sometimes have cross-purposes; it can sneak up on individuals with nothing to do with the original drama. Just as we all carry with us the sin of Adam and Eve, so too an ordinary person, encountered in the street, can be the scapegoat for a fault of which he or she was not personally guilty. It is precisely because no one is free from sin or guilt that anyone can be called to account.

I had enjoyed the cigarette I had lit at the end of that memorable day as never before in my life, at least I could remember. I retired to my room and fell into a deep sleep. Shortly before, the operations center of the Police had called me back, explaining in a few words what had happened in my house, stating they considered me extraneous to the facts but, for purely formal obligation, I would be called to testify in these days, also to acquire the information in my possession.

The next morning, after a good night's sleep, the first thing I did was go to the newsstand to buy newspapers, both local and national. All reported the news, reserving more or less ample space.

"A well-known real estate agent from Recanati was using the properties left at his disposal by the legitimate owners to organize sex and drug parties for wealthy personalities linked to culture and politics. Caught in the act by the Police of the local station, who were able to make excellent arrests", this was the headline in the Corriere della Sera, which was followed by a detailed paragraph.

The article that gave me the most satisfaction appeared in the Macerata local news page of the Resto del Carlino. The article was full-page and showed the photos, complete with the names and surnames of the people, founded by the police in the "Erotic Parties Cottage". The article did not spare sarcastic punches on the fact that politicians and personalities however in sight cannot abstain from certain vices. Here, the ambition of a former Prime Minister, since in the house there were a politician and an underage prostitute, was obvious. To make a long story short, the guests, invited and entertained by Mrs. Carla Caporalini, owner of an important real estate agency, could use drugs, even hard drugs, in abundance, they could have sex with each other or take advantage of the services offered by young prostitutes, procured by Antonio Zocchi, known in the underworld under the pseudonym Delirium. Drug dealing and exploitation of child prostitution were the serious charges for the latter. According to the investigators, having caught him at the party had been a very lucky shot. It was a long time that Police and Carabinieri were after him, without ever catching him. The real estate agent was also accused of embezzlement, aggravated fraud, and criminal association. Leonardo Gerbilli was arrested on charges of possession for profit of child pornography and, he too, for criminal association. He was considered an accomplice of Caporalini, who organized the parties and called his photographer friend for the video shooting. The hard material thus obtained would have been used to blackmail those who appeared or uploaded on paid porn sites. Lighter the accusations for the participants in the parties, which however were deceived by the trio Zocchi - Gerbilli - Caporalini. There were various charges for possession of narcotics, aiding and abetting and public indecency for the well-known writer Aurora Centofanti, for the writer and politician Paolo Biondi and - hear hear - for Chief Inspector Tonino Della Valle, originally from Recanati, but in force at the Porta Nuova Police Station in Turin, waiting for a promotion to Commissioner, which would never have arrived. A young Senegalese woman, A. H., just 15 years old, was entrusted to social services. She had been forced into prostitution since the age of 12 as soon as she arrived in Italy.

Now it was a matter of finding a suitable structure protecting her and preventing her from falling back into that abyss from which she had fortunately been saved.

Four years had passed since that fateful evening. I had moved to Ancona, in an elegant apartment in the center of town, a short distance from the port. I lived comfortably without having to work, thanks to my being a plaintiff in the trial against Carla Caporalini. The Prosecutor recognized that I had left my villa in good faith in the full availability of the Real Estate Agency, which, without my knowledge, had carried out the work to create the premises where the VIP parties were held. Therefore, at the trial, I was awarded compensation by the Real Estate Agency Caporalini, in essence by Carla, about seven hundred thousand euros. Having been released from jail after a couple of years, Carla had practically found herself reduced to a pauper, with no one to turn to, nor a home to take refuge in. Everyone had turned their backs on her, both relatives and friends. Holding justice responsible for her failure, one morning she went to the square in front of the Carabinieri barracks, doused herself with gasoline and set herself on fire. Rescued by the same soldiers, who had extinguished the flames with fire extinguishers, she was transported by helicopter to the burn center in Verona, where she died after two days, without ever regaining consciousness. She had thus met the end I had reserved for her in my dream.

Tonino had been dismissed from the police force and, no longer having a job, wandered the streets of Turin with bums and drunks. Since he no longer had an income, he had been homeless, living by his wits, getting drunk and sometimes taking drugs. One morning they found his body in a large oleander bush, in a park on the outskirts of Turin. The case was filed as "death by overdose", but no light was ever shed on the actual causes of his death, suicide, settling of accounts for not having paid the dose to the pusher, who knows? Nobody cared about him anymore.

Aurora Centofanti and Paolo Biondi seemed to have risen from their ashes. After a period of silence, Centofanti had published novels again and, thanks to the notoriety given to her by the affair, she had signed a good contract with a well-known publishing house, with which she undertook to publish a novel every three months for the series dedicated to eroticism. She had become good at the genre and her books were at the top of the charts.

As for Paolo, the saying that a politician is a turncoat and, since time immemorial, always tries to get on the bandwagon of the winners, suited his way of being perfectly. Dumped by his party, he wandered around Ancona looking for new political connections and finally found some. He promoted himself as the founder of a civic list and stood in the local elections for Mayor of Ancona. He didn't win, but he was still a prominent figure in the city. I had kept an eye on him, and I had often seen him having an aperitif or a coffee sitting at a table outside a bar near the "Fountain of the thirteen spouts"[3], sometimes alone, sometimes with businessmen or politicians.

After having stopped ringing for a few moments, the cell phone, inside the bag at the foot of the bed, resumed its insistent sound. I made a superhuman effort and, groping, I retrieved it.

«Manu, it's Paolo. I need to see you again. A damned need to see you again, after what happened last night».

Following my course of action, I should have answered him that absolutely nothing had happened, but instead: «Vicolo del Pesco number 13, on the doorbell you see my name written».

As I waited anxiously for the doorbell to ring, I realized at that very moment Emanuela "La Capricciosa" was dead forever. The Emanuela who had to satisfy her every whim no longer existed. Only Emanuela Brandimarti remained, a fragile woman who needed affection, love, human warmth, consolation for her defeats and relief from her fears. And the only person able to make her finally feel like the real "Emanuela" was about to ring her doorbell.

I had lost, yes, after four years Paolo was the winner again. But now it was okay.

Emanuela, December 31, 2014

---

[3] Famous Renaissance monument situated in the Historic Center of Ancona (Translator's note)

Sommario

Recommended price

€ 12,90 (Europe and Euro zone)

$ 13,50 (U.S.A.)

* 9 7 8 8 8 3 5 4 3 6 8 5 0 *